MURDER
AT THE CASTLE

First published in Great Britain in 2024 by
Old Street Publishing Ltd
Notaries House, Exeter EX1 1AJ

www.oldstreetpublishing.co.uk

Published in Germany by Rowohlt Verlag

ISBN 978-1-91308-346-5
Ebook ISBN 978-1-91308-347-2

The right of David Safier to be identified as the author of this work
has been asserted by him in accordance with the Copyright, Designs
and Patents Act 1988.

10 9 8 7 6 5 4 3 2 1

A CIP catalogue record for this title is available from
the British Library.

Printed and bound in Great Britain

MURDER
AT THE CASTLE

A MISS MERKEL MYSTERY

DAVID SAFIER
Translated by Jamie Bulloch

For Marion, the love of my life.
For Ben and Daniel, the other two shining
lights in my life.
I'm so proud of you!
And, of course, for Max too.

1

'Whew! I must have a little sit-down!' said Angela, and sat down on a weathered bench by a narrow gravel path with a magnificent view of the lake: the Dumpfsee. She wiped the sweat from her brow with the small handkerchief the Dalai Lama had given her. If only she could say she'd been hiking for hours in the unbearable heat of summer, rather than taking a short stroll in pleasant May sunshine. After all those years in Berlin, when the only time she would hit ten thousand steps per day was pacing up and down in her vast office during the pandemic, she was not in great shape. It was going to be some time before her body, victim of around three thousand state banquets, approached anything like fitness again.

Angela gazed at the Dumpfsee. The small lake was charming in just the ordinary way she liked. There was the perfect proportion of reeds and they wafted elegantly in a perfectly mild breeze. The water was a perfect blue, while the flight of the birds was more graceful than any ballet she'd ever seen. And Angela had seen a lot of ballets in the course of her state visits around the world. It was one of the greatest feats of her life to have stayed awake beside the president of China through all seven hours of a Beijing opera – and this despite being seriously jet-lagged.

Here on this bench, by this lake, in this weather, she didn't miss Berlin at all, even if she hadn't quite got used to life in her new home of Klein-Freudenstadt. Not that there was anything surprising about that. After all, she'd only been here for six weeks. She'd taken a few walks through the village – which was charming in the same modest way as the lake – but she didn't feel at home yet. She couldn't help wondering whether she ever would.

What if she started to crave her old hectic life in Berlin? This was her husband's biggest fear, and secretly hers too. She had made him a solemn promise that they would enjoy a peaceful retirement together. For decades he'd had to take a back-seat role – could their marriage survive if she were to break her promise?

'Is everything alright, darling?' asked Achim. Her husband's real name was Joachim, but as a student he'd decided that Achim was a cool nickname (which of course it wasn't, but then he was a quantum chemist). Now he stood in front of her in a white, short-sleeved shirt and blue cropped trousers that exposed his short, hairy legs. On his feet was a pair of grey walking boots. His cluelessness about fashion was one of the things Angela adored about her husband. She also loved his total honesty: he simply wasn't capable of lying. She often found herself wondering why all men weren't like Achim, but she never wondered for long: if they were, the human race would never have survived.

'Darling, I asked you a question.' He was always worrying about her.

'Everything's fine, Muffin. I'm just feeling a bit hot.'

From his rucksack, which he'd had since East German days, Achim took an old water bottle, from which his father had drunk before East Germany had even existed.

The water always tasted metallic. Still, Angela found it refreshing.

'Maybe you should try a new outfit?'

Angela was dressed the same way she had been throughout her years as chancellor: in black cloth trousers and one of her many colourful blazers – today's was green. The hiking clothes she'd bought five years ago were too tight, and in any case they were still languishing in one of the many unpacked removal boxes.

'When we go to Templin at the weekend, I'll get something more suitable.' There was no way she was going to buy anything on the internet. Thanks to the endless briefings from cyber-security experts in her former life, Angela knew far too much about what happened to the data of online customers. Anyway, what business of Amazon's was her dress size?

'Whatever you say, darling,' Achim replied. It was a phrase he frequently resorted to, and one that he found made life much easier.

'Ahem... Putin has made a mess,' announced a voice behind them. It belonged to an imposing man, well over six feet tall and sporting a crew cut, sunglasses and a black suit whose jacket was buttoned up to disguise a slight paunch. This was Mike, Angela's 45-year-old bodyguard. Only six weeks ago the mere mention of the P-word would have been enough to give her a sleepless night, but now she just fished a small poo bag from her blazer pocket. For this Putin wasn't the Russian president, but a small pug with a black splodge over his left eye. Achim had got him from an animal shelter and given him to

Angela on the day she retired. With the help of this cute little creature, she was hoping to get over her fear of dogs. She'd named him Putin because the real version had once let his large black Labrador loose on her in a ploy to take advantage of her phobia.

'I can pick it up if you like,' said Mike.

Angela was highly skilled at detecting when someone was making a genuine offer, and it was clear to her that Mike was not.

'That's very kind of you,' she said, holding out the small black plastic bag.

'Em… of course… my pleasure…' No doubt the man would have been less fazed by an Islamist terrorist – after all, he had been trained to reduce the fiercest attacker to a snivelling heap with a single blow. He was on the point of taking the bag when Angela bent down and said, 'Don't worry, I'm used to clearing up Putin's messes.'

She looked around. There was never a bin nearby when you needed one.

'Shall I take it?' asked Achim, who was not a man easily disgusted. 'Those who love doggies carry their loggies.'

'What have I told you about your little jokes, Achim?'

'Keep them to myself?'

'Correct.'

Angela stroked his cheek fondly with her free hand, then turned to Mike. 'Is there a shorter way back to the village? I want to pick up some apples for a cake and the shops will be shutting soon.'

The early closing times were just one of many differences between Klein-Freudenstadt and Berlin. Angela wasn't sure whether to find them endearingly quaint or just plain irritating.

'Apple cake?' said Mike.

Angela knew her bodyguard loved cakes and rated her baking skills highly. At the same time he was worried about losing his athletic physique. Since being assigned to the Merkels he'd gained 2 kilos and 358 grams, despite rigorous physical training. Achim had no such issues. He could eat whatever he liked without putting on a gram. It was one of her husband's qualities Angela had always been slightly envious of.

Ever since coming to Klein-Freudenstadt she'd baked a cake almost every day: strawberry, pear, plum. Whatever the fruit stalls in the market square had to offer. Baking wasn't just a way to fill the hours that, until a few weeks ago, she'd spent in meetings – it was a genuine passion. In another life she might have been a pastry chef rather than a scientist and a politician. In a parallel universe – and as a physicist she endorsed the theory that such things existed – there might well be an Angela who happily spent all day long making butter cake and quark doughnuts. Perhaps there was even a universe in which she could eat all the cakes she wanted without putting on any weight.

'We can take a short cut through the woods,' said Mike.

Angela set off purposefully, followed by Achim, Mike and Putin, who despite his short, bandy legs could easily keep up with his mistress.

They'd barely gone one hundred metres when they heard the sound of thundering hooves, followed soon afterwards by the appearance of horse and rider. She couldn't know it at the time, but this was Angela's first encounter with the man whose dead body she would find in a dungeon only hours later.

2

'Whoah, Ferdinand!

The most surprising thing about Baron Philipp von Baugenwitz wasn't his black stallion, whose thorough-bred physique would have given the other runners at Ascot an instant inferiority complex. Nor the fact that this magnificent beast went by the incongruous name of Ferdinand. It was that Philipp von Baugenwitz was clad in a suit of armour.

'And I thought I'd seen every nutter under the sun,' muttered Mike, having quickly identified the knight on horseback as harmless.

Her years in politics had taught Angela that there was always a bigger nutter just around the corner. But even she couldn't hide a degree of astonishment. Meanwhile Putin sought refuge from the horse behind her legs and Achim raised an eyebrow. It was a skill he'd learned as a child from Commander Spock in *Star Trek*.

'It really is you!' said the helmet. 'Ever since I heard you'd moved to our lovely little village I've been looking forward to meeting you.'

Angela deduced from his voice that the man in the helmet was in his early fifties. She noted approvingly that he had the good manners not to mention the poo bag in her hand, although he must have spotted it.

'I expect you're wondering why I'm in a suit of armour.'

'The question had crossed my mind.'

'This evening I'm hosting a medieval wine festival at my castle and I wanted to see how it felt. It belonged to my ancestor Balduin. And, I have to say, it feels really, really good! I'm definitely going to wear it this evening. You must have seen the posters for the festival?'

'I have. And I received the flyer too.' This had stuck in her memory because she'd been handed the paper by a teenager with dyed-blue hair who was so fixated by her mobile phone that she hadn't clocked who Angela was. The last time someone had failed to recognise her was decades ago. At first it had felt strange, then liberating.

'May I count on your presence this evening?'

Angela and Achim had planned to settle into their new timber-framed cottage before venturing further afield. But how was she going to settle into in her new house if she didn't also settle into the village it was part of? And where better to start than at a festival attended by most of the village?

'It sounds interesting,' she said. She heard her bodyguard give a faint sigh behind her. It was his night off and he'd been hoping to treat himself to a nice drink in Aladdin's Gin. This was the classiest bar in Klein-Freudenstadt, and also the only bar in Klein-Freudenstadt. Apart from that there was just the village inn, which was called Village Inn. Angela knew that if Mike had to keep an eye on her at the festival he wouldn't allow himself even a sip of wine. No drinking on duty. It was hardly surprising that he was less than thrilled.

Angela looked at Achim, who again raised an eyebrow – the other one this time. Over the years he'd really perfected the art. She remembered that she'd promised him they'd watch *La Traviata* on live transmission from the New York Metropolitan Opera, for which he'd specifically bought a new large-screen television (on special offer of course). Angela recalled his efforts to set up the remote control, as he proved once again that quantum chemists are totally clueless when it comes to everyday technology. It was only when Putin trotted all over it with his little paws that the gadget started to work.

So, neither Achim nor Mike was exactly head over heels with excitement at the prospect of the wine festival that evening. In her husband's case this was just as well, since he would certainly crick his neck if he tried to put his head anywhere near his heels. Yet Angela was reluctant to turn down the baron's invitation. She was curious, and even had high hopes that she'd enjoy this event in her new neighbourhood.

'You won't regret it. I hope to see you this evening!' said the baron tinnily, and rode off.

'And I hope not,' muttered Achim.

'It might be fun,' said Angela.

'But we were going to watch *La Traviata*!'

'We still can,' said Angela. 'There's something called a record button. I'm sure Putin could find it.'

'Ha ha,' was Achim's reply. He was many things, but quick-witted wasn't one of them.

'Come on, Muffin. Let's see how people party here.' Angela employed this pet name strategically. That is, whenever she needed to get her husband to do things he didn't want to. A well-timed 'Muffin' could make him join in with the WAGs' activities at G7 conferences, even after Melania Trump had replaced Michelle Obama.

Still, Achim hesitated.

Angela deployed a smile. 'Aren't you at all curious to see what the face beneath the helmet looks like?'

'I could google that,' said Achim.

'I'll do it now,' said Mike, whipping out his mobile again. 'And if I can't find a picture of him online I'll ask my colleagues at the Federal Police Bureau. And if they don't have one they could hack into his mobile or send a drone with a high-resolution camera to—'

'We will all see him in the flesh tonight,' said Angela, laying down the law like the pro she was. Ignoring the scowls of the two men, she bent down to pat Putin's head. 'And you're going to get a yummy bit of chicken this evening.'

Putin was delighted. 'Chicken' was one of the sounds he understood, like 'Sit', 'Lie down' and 'Yes, you can sit on the sofa even though Achim is raising an eyebrow.'

Angela set off, poo bag still in hand. As she walked, she pondered which blazer she should wear to the festival.

3

Over the past six weeks the people of Klein-Freudenstadt had gradually become accustomed to Angela's presence. Of course they noticed the former chancellor when she turned up in the old market square – as now with hus-

9

band, pug and bodyguard – but they no longer queued for selfies with her. They rarely gawped or whispered comments, kind or (as had sometimes been the case) otherwise. Within two or three months, Angela was sure they would be completely used to her.

After finally depositing the black bag in a bin, she wandered through the small market. Even to a woman like Angela, who didn't go overboard with sentimentality, it looked idyllic. There were ten stalls selling produce from the surrounding Uckermark region: cheese, organic meat, fruit and vegetables, honey and even wine from the baron's vineyard. Angela bypassed this – no doubt she'd be sampling the rare vintage later at the festival – and instead made for an organic fruit stall attended by a jovial-looking, rather chubby woman in her late forties, dressed in blue dungarees and a blue-and-white headscarf.

'Good afternoon,' she said. 'I'd like seven apples, please.'
'Take eight!' said the stallholder.
'Does that make it cheaper per apple?'
'No, but you'd have one more.'
Angela couldn't help laughing. 'I'll take eight, then.'
'You won't regret it.'

While Angela was being served, Achim waited at the wine stall. He had taken the panting dog into his arms. Putin was in even worse shape than his mistress. If things went on like this they'd both have to go on a diet.

Achim was probably finding out all about viticulture in the Uckermark. Her husband loved doing this: asking endless questions and then not buying anything. It was astonishing that he'd never been banned from any shop.

Mike stood a few metres away, scanning the market square for danger. Angela thought he might as well save himself the bother. What could possibly happen to her here? The idea of an assassin in a sleepy place like Klein-Freudenstadt was absurd. Besides, who would benefit from killing her? Angela had made a conscious decision to step out of the public eye, and was determined to keep it this way. She had no intention of annoying her successors by appearing on talk shows, writing newspaper columns or giving lectures. Nor did she feel the need, unlike certain other ex-chancellors, to sit on endless supervisory boards, lucrative as they might be. What was the point of earning more money than a normal person could ever require?

Angela was about to tell her bodyguard to relax when a pregnant woman approached her. She was black, perhaps in her mid-thirties, and was wearing a loose-fitting, green-and-pink spring dress. In her long, smooth hair was a green headband. Angela hadn't come across many immigrants, of any generation, in Klein-Freudenstadt. There was the man who ran the Italian ice-cream parlour, who came from Serbia; the owner of Müller's butcher's, who was from Taiwan; and the sales assistant in the stationery shop, who was from somewhere near Stuttgart. Angela assumed the woman must have some connection with one of East Germany's socialist brother countries: Mozambique, Ethiopia, Benin…

'Hello. May I have a word?' the woman asked with a friendly smile.

11

'Of course,' Angela said, returning the smile. 'What can I do for you?'

'It's me who can do something for you! My name is Marie Horstmann and I run the tourist office here.'

Angela hid her surprise at the woman's Teutonic name. 'Klein-Freudenstadt has a tourist office?'

'Yes, but it's only open for two hours twice a week. Unfortunately the job doesn't pay enough to live on.'

'So what are you going to do for me?'

'Well, I can offer you a guided tour of the village and tell you everything you need to know about it that you won't find on Wikipedia.'

'Half of the Wikipedia entry is a warning not to get Klein-Freudenstadt mixed up with Klein-Freudenstedt in Baden-Württemberg!'

'True! I assume whoever wrote it was led astray by their SatNav.'

Angela nodded. It was a plausible theory. 'It's a plausible theory,' she said.

Marie pointed at the village church. 'For example, I can tell you which pastor drank all the communion wine then spent the rest of the day ringing the bells without any clothes on. And why the black stone in front of the church is called the *Stone of Tears*. Not to mention how Balduin von Baugenwitz died in his suit of armour.'

Angela winced. So the baron had been wearing the very suit of armour his ancestor had died in. Either the man had a morbid streak or he lacked imagination.

'That does all sound very exciting.' None of the things the young woman had mentioned had been in the dossier

12

on the village Angela had been sent by the intelligence service. It was while reading through this dossier at her desk in the chancellery that she had first had the thought: this ordinary place could suit me just perfectly!

'Does tomorrow afternoon at four work for you?' asked Marie.

'I have no other plans,' said Angela, uttering these words for the first time since the previous millennium. 'My husband and bodyguard will come along too.'

'Three tickets sold. A new record!' beamed Marie.

Achim approached. 'I have some good news,' he said.

'I love good news,' said Angela. She had learned from experience just how rare it was.

'We *can* watch *La Traviata* live after all.'

'Did you get the day wrong?' Angela couldn't help sounding surprised even as she realised this was impossible. Achim never made mistakes when it came to dates, numbers and facts.

'No, the performance is tonight. But we don't have to go to the wine festival.'

'No?'

'The wine they make at the castle is mediocre. To put it generously.'

'Muffin, we aren't going to the wine festival for the wine.'

'We aren't?' Achim was confused.

'It's about meeting our neighbours. And while we're on the subject, this is Marie Horstmann. She runs the Klein-Freudenstadt tourist office.'

'Pleased to meet you. Achim Sauer – Sauer as in sweet, only the opposite.'

13

'Pleased to meet you too,' said Marie.

'You must be coming to the festival this evening?' said Angela. To her consternation, Marie's face, until then so cheerful, hardened at a stroke. Angela even fancied she detected a shudder.

'No,' she said.

'Are you doing something else, *like us*?' asked Achim.

'We aren't doing anything else,' said Angela, turning to Marie. 'See you tomorrow then,' she said kindly, to give her a chance to get away without further distress.

'Yes... four p.m. on the dot,' said Marie. She tried and failed to produce a smile. 'See you then.'

'And I thought *I* hated bad wine!' said Achim.

'I don't think Marie is avoiding the festival because of the quality of the wine.'

'It would be perfectly logical if she were.'

'I fear she has a deeper reason.' Angela wondered what had made the pregnant woman shudder. Was there a husband who didn't let her go out? Or was it something about the festival itself? Would somebody be there who she didn't want to bump into?

Angela decided to broach the question discreetly during tomorrow's tour. She instinctively liked Marie, and was eager to help her in any way she could.

4

Angela had donned her favourite red blazer, the one she'd worn to the 2014 World Cup final. Achim, who could scarcely remember who had won that game, let alone who the opposition had been, was wearing his best and only suit. He'd bought it in 1997, the first time he'd had to accompany Angela to an official function. The occasion had confirmed his hypothesis that he wouldn't find such events remotely fun.

The three of them – Angela, Achim and Mike – were in the living room of the Merkels' timber-framed house, built in 1789. It had low ceilings, and according to Achim's calculations Mike hit his head on the beams on average 3.73 times per day. Still, it was a cosy place. They had acquired much of the previous owners' furniture, including nineteenth-century cupboards, a rustic dining table with even more rustic chairs, and an insanely comfortable armchair. Achim had envisaged spending long hours in it reading his books on particle theory, but Putin had turned the armchair into his favourite sleeping place.

I'm going to have to work out for an extra half hour tomorrow,' sighed Mike, polishing off his third slice of Angela's freshly baked apple cake.

'I'm so sorry,' said Angela, who in fact derived a certain wicked pleasure in undermining the man's iron self-discipline.

She covered the cake, while Achim loaded the dishwasher according to a complex mathematical system that his wife never questioned. Not only did she have no desire to listen to him expound his method – which supposedly saved them every 12.7th washing cycle – but more importantly, she didn't want to do anything to shake Achim's conviction that only he could load the dishwasher perfectly, thus freeing her from this task for the rest of her life.

'Should I give the leftovers to those two homeless guys in the village again?' asked Mike.

'Of course.'

Mike grinned. 'They've put on a few pounds too over the last few weeks.'

You couldn't tell by looking at him, but Mike had a big heart. He was divorced, and when interviewing him for the job Angela had been swung by how utterly devoted he was to his young daughter in Kiel. Another bonus was that, unlike the other candidates, he didn't look as though he'd slaughter a puppy without batting an eyelid if given the order to do so. She had no wish to subject herself or her darling pet to men like that.

She glanced over at Putin, who was just curling up in his basket – insofar as a pug could curl up. When he finally found his ideal position his guts let out a sigh of comfort that everyone in the room could hear. And smell.

'I think,' said Angela, 'that is the signal for us to leave.'

Mike and Achim were only too happy to agree. The three of them went outside, took a deep breath of fresh air and set off towards the castle. As she trotted along the cobbled street with its quaint houses, Angela realised how much she was looking forward to meeting her fellow villagers. She was sure it would help her feel at home. And the sooner she felt at home, the sooner that little part of her which longed to go back to Berlin – something she hid from Achim – would be silenced.

5

Their route took them past St Petri Church and out of the village onto a little-used country road. Up ahead was the seventeenth-century Castle Baugenwitz on its hilltop. The white masonry gleamed in the late-afternoon sun, and the scarlet roofs shone vibrantly.

Angela, Achim and Mike joined the crowd of people walking up the tree-lined drive towards the castle. A tractor chugged past. On it sat four farmers, along with the fruit-seller from the market, all wearing grim expressions. A large banner was fixed to the back of the machine: DON'T SELL OUR LAND!

Naturally Angela had read in the intelligence dossier that the baron was in dire financial straits. It was only thanks to all the subsidies he had received that the castle gleamed so brightly. The hotel business that was supposed to cover the maintenance costs had been shut down after huge losses. The small vineyard and the rent from the farmers barely made a dent in the deficit the property was running. Von Baugenwitz was forever assuring the local press that the castle and estate were not up for sale, and that he wished to preserve the centuries-old tradition of his family in the Uckermark. Not long ago, however, a lucrative offer had come in from an eccentric American electric car manufacturer, who planned to turn the estate into a home with a golf course – his seventeenth home with a golf course. The villagers suspected that the baron's attachment to his ancestral estate might not be robust enough to resist the lure of the dollar.

When Angela, Achim and Mike arrived at the castle

gate, the farmers were setting up their protest: banners, flyers and a megaphone that whined when it was switched on and gave feedback every five seconds. Undeterred, one particularly irate-looking farmer yelled into it: 'The Uckermark belongs to us! The Uckermark belongs to us!'

'Strictly speaking,' said Achim, 'what that man is saying is not true. Unfortunately much of the land doesn't belong to the Uckermarkers, but to a small number of private individuals such as the baron, or to the state.'

'I don't think you should mention that to the protesters.'

'Why not?'

'What did I always tell my ministers?'

'Nobody likes a smart-arse?'

'Precisely.' Noticing that Mike was eyeing the protesters suspiciously, Angela said to him, 'I don't think there's any danger here.'

'No danger? There's danger lurking everywhere! Like in Johannesburg when that dog – the one that seemed so cute – suddenly attacked the foreign minister and made a huge hole in his trousers, so you could see his test—'

'Mike!' Angela interrupted him.

'Too much information?'

'Too much information.'

Angela went over to where the protesters were gathered. 'May I have a flyer?' she asked the friendly fruit-seller.

'Take two.'

'Because then I'll have one more?'

'You're a fast learner.'

The two women grinned at each other. It might be

nice to get to know this woman better, thought Angela. Maybe she liked baking apple cake too? A baking friend would certainly help her settle in.

A friend…

Angela had never had a best friend. Not even in primary school, where the other girls often made fun of her. *Yuck, yuck, tut-tut, Angela's got a bowl cut.*

Achim had Tommy, his best friend since university, who he played Scrabble with via Skype every couple of days. But the women with whom Angela had spent the past few decades were defence ministers, prime ministers and bureau chiefs. No real friend could be found amongst those. Not that it had ever bothered her. Achim had been more than enough of a best friend to fill her meagre spare time. But now what? What would she do with herself when Achim and Tommy went off on their annual three-week hiking tour in the Alps? Angela could already see herself paying secret visits to Berlin to avoid vegetating on her own in Klein-Freudenstadt. Or she could stay and bake cakes with a real friend. That was a better option.

'What do you think my name is?' asked the woman. 'I'll give you three guesses.'

Angela thought about it.

'Just please don't say Mandy!' said the woman.

'Sandy? Or Candy?' joked Angela.

'No!' the woman laughed.

'Brandy?' When she felt at ease, Angela enjoyed a bit of silliness as much as the next person.

The fruit-seller laughed even louder. 'No, I'm called Angela too!'

'Really?'

'Really!'

Now they both laughed.

Achim interrupted their fun. 'Shall we go to the wine festival?'

'While you're at the castle,' said the other Angela, 'please tell his noble Lordship that he mustn't sell the estate. It's not just that our livelihoods depend on it, the environment would suffer too. The Yank wants to drain the lake behind the castle, but it's an important spawning ground for lots of species.'

'I'll see what I can do,' promised Angela without really promising anything. It was a simple manoeuvre, almost second nature after so many years in politics.

She, Achim and Mike went through the gate into the courtyard. On the back of the flyer was a photograph of the friendly fruit-seller. She was indeed called Angela. Angela Kessler. And not only was she a farmer and fruit-seller, she was also a music teacher. And on top of that, she was deputy district chair of the hard-right *Alternative für Deutschland* party!

So much for baking cakes together with her new friend.

6

The castle courtyard was teeming with Klein-Freuden-stadters being served wine by men in medieval Harlequin costumes, and small wild boar sausages by women, also in medieval outfits. Angela knew she wouldn't get the barbecue smell out of her red blazer in a hurry. She glanced at Mike, who had been momentarily mesmerised by a sausage. He was probably wondering how many extra minutes of exercise it would add to tomorrow's workout.

At the rear of the courtyard, men with long beards were playing a version of 'La Cucaracha' on historical instruments. It wasn't exactly an easy listen. The guests, numbering two hundred perhaps, were having a splendid time. And in the centre of it all, wearing the suit of armour in which his ancestor had perished, stood the baron himself. Beside him was an attractive blonde, early thirties, in a tight-fitting black dress that was not remotely medieval. In a single, elegant movement she downed a glass of champagne and replaced it jauntily on the tray of a passing Harlequin while simultaneously grabbing another with her free hand.

'You came!' the baron called out delightedly, teetering and rattling over.

The young woman in the black dress followed, swigging champagne. Her ring, with its super-sized diamond, suggested she was his wife. Just as the baron was about to speak, she said under her breath: 'Take that stupid thing off!' It was clearly meant as a command.

'You're quite right,' said her husband, freeing his head from the heavy helmet. A greying man in his early fifties appeared. Angela noted with surprise that he looked like a cross between Roger Moore and Norbert Röttgen.

'May I introduce to you my wife, Alexa von Baugenwitz,' he said with a smile straight out of a toothpaste ad. Doubtless over the years it had bewitched many a woman.

21

'No doubt better known to you,' said the baroness with a dazzling smile of her own, 'as Alexa Morgen.'

'No. The name means nothing to me,' said Achim, who would not have been a strong candidate for the diplomatic service.

'From *Red Roses*,' prompted the woman.

Angela, who was well aware that her husband was as clueless about *Red Roses* as he was about Red Noses or for that matter anything relating to popular culture, said: 'It's a TV series.'

'My darling Alexa was in it until I rode to her rescue and made her my wife,' said the baron.

'Rescue? I was the star!' The forced smile failed to mask the anger she felt at her husband's condescension. Alexa Morgen clearly believed she was a great actress.

'Whatever you say, dearest,' said the baron. Angela half-expected him to pat his wife's head.

'I played Dr Beate Borg, the doctor adored by all her female patients even though she has an alcohol problem.'

Here at least was a point where actress and role could come together.

'The doctor *abhorred* by all her female patients, more like,' said her husband. It was obvious that he thought he'd made a brilliant witticism.

'Don't laugh too hard or your teeth might fall out,' said his wife.

The baron stopped laughing. 'You shouldn't drink so much,' he said.

'There are one or two things you shouldn't do either!'

'Perhaps we could discuss this later?'

'Why not now, in front of all these good people?'

Angela moved to de-escalate. 'But perhaps not all these good people want to hear about it,' she said.

'I certainly don't,' said Achim.

'The thing is, my *darling* husband here—'

Just then a female voice interrupted. 'Philipp! It's time for you to open the festival!'

All heads turned towards a dark-haired woman around fifty. Her black trouser suit and clipboard suggested she was in charge of the evening's festivities.

'In that case I'd better open the festival,' said the baron, clanking noisily off in his armour without saying goodbye. His eagerness to escape the unpleasant scene his wife had created was only too apparent. Also without another word, Alexa departed in search of more champagne.

'I'm sorry you had to witness that,' said the woman with the clipboard.

'It's not your fault,' said Angela. The woman looked smart and educated, with a stylishness you wouldn't necessarily expect to find in Klein-Freudenstadt. Angela had sensed right away that she was her equal in intelligence; her instinct for such things rarely let her down. Maybe she should suggest meeting up with her? If not to bake, then to discuss Goethe, Rilke or even Shakespeare over a cup of tea.

'May I introduce myself? Katharina von Baugenwitz.'

'I thought that other woman was the baron's wife,' said Achim.

'I was his first wife.'

23

'Do you all live here together?'

'It's a big castle. If you want to it's easy to avoid one another for weeks on end. My apartment is in the west wing. As is my office – I look after the business side of things.'

Angela wondered whether she was involved in the sale of the castle to the American car manufacturer.

'I'll give you a little tour afterwards if you like.'

'That would be lovely,' said Angela. She was keen to get to know this woman better.

'Wonderful. We can do it in half an hour. But may I ask you something first?'

'Of course.'

'With your contacts in the ministry of justice there's a matter you might be able to help me with.'

Angela had moved away from Berlin precisely to avoid conversations of this kind, but she put on a brave smile and once again promised something without promising anything. Still, she was disappointed. She no longer felt like having a cup of tea with this woman.

'Pia!' Katharina von Baugenwitz motioned to a teenager with blue hair and a black leather jacket. It was the young girl who'd given Angela the flyer for the wine festival yesterday without recognising her.

'What?' asked the girl in a tone of thorough boredom.

'Please would you take a photo of me and this lady for our website?'

'If you like.' The girl sounded about as enthusiastic as David Cameron had when they were discussing the free movement of people in the European Union.

'Pia is my daughter from my first marriage,' Katharina von Baugenwitz said.

'Don Quixote's daughter, then?' asked Achim.

'No, Philipp was my second husband.' Katharina's tone made her feelings about the marriage clear. 'My first husband died in a car accident.'

'I'm very sorry,' Achim said.

'I'm very sorry too,' said Angela, to the blue-haired girl as well. Without replying, she began to fiddle with her smartphone. It was as if her father's death was no concern of hers. 'That must have been difficult for your daughter,' said Angela, turning back to the mother.

'Yes, she worshipped her father.' There was a tremor in Katharina's voice. 'But she knows I'm there for her. And that I'd do anything for her. Anything!'

Angela looked at the girl. It couldn't have been easy when her mother had married Philipp, making him her stepfather. Since her mother's divorce poor Pia had lost two fathers, albeit in different ways.

'Can't you take your eyes off that thing?' said Katharina, clearly wanting to change the subject.

'I can,' said Pia, without doing it.

'In the past,' sighed Katharina, 'you had to drag her out of the library, but now she's forgotten what a book is.'

'So do you want me to take a photo or not?'

'My daughter is an excellent photographer. She's an influencer, you know.'

'What's the difference between influenza and—' said Achim.

'Muffin, what did I say about COVID jokes?'

'That you never, ever want to hear another one.'

'Precisely.'

'You call your husband *Muffin*? For real?' said Pia.

Angela was not amused. 'Are you going to take a picture or are we going to talk about our pet names?'

'Let's talk about your pet names. So how does it work? Do you ever say: *Kiss me, Muffin*?'

Mike, who'd come over bearing a sausage, failed to suppress a guffaw. Angela gave him one of her looks, and he swiftly regained his composure.

'Or how about,' continued the blue-haired girl, '*give it to me, Muffin*?'

Mike gave a loud, sausagey snort.

'I think we'll leave the photo for now,' said Angela, moving off.

Katharina turned angrily to her daughter. 'Pia! What were you thinking!'

'What's the big deal?'

'That woman could be useful to us!'

Overhearing this exchange, Angela thought that maybe getting to know the people of Klein-Freudenstadt wouldn't be so much fun after all.

7

The baron stepped onto a small podium set up in the castle courtyard. He'd put the helmet back on and now said into a microphone, 'Hail, my dear subjects!'

The reaction of the crowd was one of bewilderment mixed with hilarity.

'Lose the helmet!' shouted his current wife, her speech already slightly slurred. Her predecessor, Katharina, still clutching the clipboard, shook her head. Angela couldn't tell whether she was more disgusted by the baron or his inebriated wife. Meanwhile, Pia stood a few metres away, filming the speech with her mobile, no doubt for the castle's social media channels.

'Oh… yes… excuse me,' said the baron. He opened the helmet's visor, but the look he shot his wife made it clear that he had no intention of taking the thing off.

He began to read from a script. 'My greeting to you was how my ancestor and founder of Baugenwitz Castle, Balduin von Baugenwitz, would have addressed you. No doubt shortly before having some of you impaled on stakes for failing to pay your tribute.'

Nobody apart from the baron found this funny.

'Or perhaps he would have had you broken on the wheel, put in an iron maiden or clubbed mercilessly with a morning star.'

The crowd began to shift uncomfortably.

'This guy's even less funny than my boss's husband,' muttered Mike.

Achim gave him a look.

Mike went red. 'Uh… Did I say that too loud?'

Angela made a mental note for the next appraisal meeting: Mike needed to understand that his deep voice carried a long way, even when he was trying to whisper.

'Life has moved on,' continued the baron, still reading from the piece of paper. 'These days the baron wouldn't lay a finger on anyone. Apart from that time we were out shooting and a stray bullet of mine may have accidentally grazed the arm of our policewoman Fräulein Amadeus.'

Now the crowd did laugh. All apart from the uniformed, red-haired woman in her late twenties who the baron now pointed to. She didn't appear amused in the slightest. Angela noticed, however, that she had clocked Mike and was sizing him up with interest. Perhaps he was her type.

'Anyway,' the baron said, buoyed up by the laughter, 'I was merely fined for that. Whereas my ancestor Balduin was poisoned with hemlock by his own wife.'

While in his suit of armour, Angela thought, putting two and two together.

'My more recent ancestors lived in greater harmony with their subjects. Wilhelm the Peaceful for example. Or Kasimir the Bird-Lover. Or Isidor… who also loved birds.'

More laughter, except from those women who were married to the baron, had been married to him, or had been shot by him.

'Just like you!' his drunken wife yelled, much to the discomfort of the assembled guests. Only the teenager with blue hair was grinning.

The baron turned red, more with anger than embarrassment. 'Maybe it would be best if I finish now,' he said. 'As the representative of the von Baugenwitz family, I'm delighted that we've been able to live back in our castle for the last thirty years, after it was snatched away from us by the illegitimate communist state. And I hereby swear to you all that I will never sell it!'

The crowd cheered. Angela turned around to see if

the fruit-seller and her fellow protesters had heard this vow. They wore sceptical expressions. The baron performed an awkward bow in his armour, while his wife, handing her glass to a waiter, hurried off into the castle.

'And now: music!' declared Philipp von Baugenwitz. The medieval band launched into a highly idiosyncratic version of 'The Macarena'. The first couples peeled away from the crowd and began to dance. Achim bobbed up and down to the music too. He had zero talent for dancing, but music always got him going.

Exhilarated by the success of his speech, the baron clanked his way across the gravel, making a beeline for Angela. 'So, how was it?' he asked smugly.

'It was remarkable,' replied Angela. She was well versed in telling diplomatic half-truths to vain men.

'Coming from a remarkable woman like yourself, that makes me happy.'

Not for the first time, Angela reflected how incredibly easy it was to flatter the male ego.

'Do you know what would give me great pleasure?'

'I'm sure you're going to tell me,' said Angela.

'I'd like to take you out.'

'Out?'

'Yes, there's a wonderful restaurant in the neighbouring village called *Entre Nous*. They specialise in candlelit dinners,' purred the baron with his toothpaste-ad smile that he clearly believed to be irresistible. 'How about it?'

Angela resisted the urge to shudder. 'Perhaps when I've settled in a bit more,' she said.

29

'I can help you settle in,' said the lord of the castle, dialling up his smile still further. 'Think about it.'

For Angela there was nothing to think about. Another reason for moving to Klein-Freudenstadt was not to have to go to dinner ever again with rich and influential men who thought they were irresistible. Still, because she knew that these sorts of men only heard what they wanted to hear, she said, 'Thinking is always good.'

'You won't regret it!' said the baron, delighted with himself, before wandering off through the dancing guests and back into the castle after his wife.

'He was flirting with you,' said Achim peevishly.

'No he wasn't.'

'A hundred percent he was,' said Mike.

Angela remembered Nicholas Sarkozy's ludicrous efforts to charm her during EU budget negotiations. These days, however, she had nothing to give away. 'Why would anyone flirt with me now?' she said.

'I don't know,' said Achim.

'That's the wrong answer,' she grinned.

Achim looked confused.

'What you meant to say was: "Because you're an intelligent, highly attractive woman."'

'Oh yes, yes… Of course you are!'

Angela smiled. She was well aware that Achim did in fact think she was the smartest and most beautiful woman in the world. He'd always been so sweetly jealous, since their earliest days at university. One time, when she was already going out with Achim, a fellow PhD student, a very sporty type, had made a move on her. Achim was furious. Squaring up to his rival, he'd said, 'If you don't leave my Angela alone, I'll—'

'You'll what?' the sporty guy had replied.

'I'll thump you. Then you'll beat me up and I'll just have to hope that Angela will still choose me.'

Which is exactly what happened. No doubt there were many men who would fight over a woman, but Achim went a step further: he loved Angela so much he would willingly submit to a thrashing for her.

'You're not really going to go out to dinner with him, are you?'

'Muffin, do you think I'm mad?'

'Is that a trick question?'

'No.'

'You know I think you're mad,' said Achim. He'd never understood why Angela had given up her scientific career.

'I'm not so mad that I'd willingly spend even a minute alone with a man like that.'

'No, you can't be that mad,' her husband conceded.

During this little exchange, Mike's attention had wandered back to the young policewoman. She was just getting a mineral water from the drinks stand.

'Why don't you go over to her?' Angela suggested.

'Erm… what?'

'Don't pretend you don't know what I'm talking about.'

'I don't have time for that sort of thing. I have to look after you.'

'And you're doing that by staring at the policewoman?'

Mike tore his gaze away from the beautiful redhead

31

and hectically looked in all directions as if there might be a few extremists amongst the dancing guests.

'There's no danger here,' said Angela.

'Do you know what my instructor used to say about phrases like that?'

'No.'

'Famous last words.'

'He must have been paranoid.'

'Not paranoid. Vigilant. An essential quality for every bodyguard.'

'Well, if you have to keep close watch over me,' said Angela mischievously, 'you'll have to accompany me as I go to get a drink.'

Mike looked nervously at the drinks stand. The police-woman was now leaning against it, holding a glass of water. 'There's another stand over there – it's less busy,' he said.

'Yes, but it's further away.'

Angela set off, with Mike in tow. Beads of sweat appeared on his brow. He would have felt more relaxed cutting the wire of a ticking bomb. Achim stayed where he was, trying and failing to memorise the sequence of moves in the Macarena. His quantum chemist's brain simply wasn't up to it.

When Angela and Mike reached the stand, she said a friendly 'Hello' to the young policewoman, followed by, 'This is Mike, my bodyguard.'

The redhead smiled bewitchingly. 'Hello,' she replied, her eyes sparkling. 'I'm Lena.'

'I'm... Mike,' said Mike. He was better at interrogating suspects than talking to attractive women.

32

'Mike, tell Lena how important it is for a bodyguard to cooperate with the local police force.'

'It's... very important,' said Mike.

'Is there anything you'd like to know?' said the policewoman with another smile, clearly trying to make it easier for Mike. She seemed to like him despite his stammering. Or perhaps because of it: it was a nice contrast with his powerful stature.

Sweating ever more profusely, Mike desperately tried to think of something to ask. All he could come up with was, 'Do you know where the loos are?'

Summoning all her powers of restraint, acquired the hard way during press conferences with Trump, Putin and many others, Angela managed not to slap her forehead.

Still smiling, Lena gestured towards the portacabins.

'Thanks,' said Mike, scuttling away.

'He's not always like that,' said Angela.

At that moment Achim came over. 'I just can't get the movements to this dance,' he announced.

'Don't expect me to show you,' said Angela.

'Why would I expect that? You're just as clumsy as I am.'

'Let me introduce Achim, my husband,' said Angela. 'The most honest person in the world.'

'Lena Amadeus,' said the policewoman. 'I'd love to stay and chat, but I've been asked by Katharina von Baugenwitz to check the rear of the castle is still burglar-proof. And because I'm here on duty, I'll have to leave as soon as the festival ends. But would you mind passing on a message to your bodyguard?'

'Not at all.'

'Tell him I'd love to meet him tomorrow evening in Aladdin's Gin.'

'Certainly!' Angela felt very pleased with herself.

The young woman left and Angela watched the merry crowd drinking and laughing. Children ran around noisily, while a few couples waltzed with various degrees of accomplishment. Everything was bathed in the golden evening light. Angela felt a warm glow in her heart. Maybe this was the right place to spend the rest of her life after all. A life in which she would discover new things about herself and Achim. The glow became so warm that she decided to embark on something new right away.

'Let's dance,' she whispered to Achim.

'What?'

'I'd like to dance with you,' she said, slightly louder this time.

'I can't dance.'

'I know that.'

'And nor can you.'

'I think we could manage a bit of rhythmical swaying.'

'That's what you said at the Vienna Opera Ball in 2001, where I trod on your toes seven times in just under five minutes.'

'True.'

'And you stepped on mine three times.'

'Sorry.'

'Love means never having to say you're sorry,' said Achim. He cried every time he watched Ryan O'Neal utter these words to Ali McGraw at the end of his favourite film, *Love Story*.

'Come on. If we keep our feet firmly on the ground we can't step on each other's toes.'

'Sounds logical.'

'So...'

'Will you give me the pleasure of the next dance?' Achim chuckled, took her hand, and guided her over to the dance floor. The couple rocked gently back and forth in the middle of the throng.

It was lovely. Why they hadn't done this ages ago? Maybe she and Achim could take dancing lessons. They would make an excellent challenge for any teacher.

As Angela swayed in rhythm with her husband, she felt for the first time properly at ease in her new home. She was too wrapped up in the moment to notice that all the villagers she'd spoken to that evening had left the castle courtyard: the baron, his wife, his ex-wife, her daughter, fruit-seller Angela and the policewoman.

8

After the dance Angela and Achim wandered across the courtyard with a spring in their step. On closer inspection, the castle was rather tatty. The paint was peeling off in several places and a number of roof tiles were missing. A few sad-looking fish swam around in the fountain, which was in urgent need of a clean. The money from East Germany's economic restructuring programme had been spent long ago, and it seemed there was nothing left for the upkeep of the place. While Angela pondered this, Achim marvelled at the roses climbing up beautiful arches and the little white-flowering plants that alone seemed to be permitted to grow amongst their thorns.

A few children came up to Angela to ask for selfies, egged on by their parents who waved sheepishly from a distance. She was happy to go along with it, realising to her surprise that she actually enjoyed having her picture taken when it wasn't part of her job. Maybe she should do a selfie with Achim? No, he hated selfies. He had a theory that he looked best from behind, and she didn't want to risk spoiling the moment by annoying him. After all, the only time they'd ever been this relaxed together was on hiking holidays in the Tyrol. But now they weren't on holiday, they were embarking on a new life. Maybe even a better one than before. An everlasting holiday, so to speak.

No sooner had Angela had this thought than the doubts returned. She'd never been one for long holidays. At some point wouldn't she start to feel bored without anything to do apart from baking, cooking and reading books? Wouldn't she long for a new occupation, like a chair at a university? If that happened Achim would definitely be disappointed. Not just disappointed, he'd feel betrayed. She'd always promised him this retirement in the Uckermark.

Angela sighed and decided she could do with a glass of wine. She guided her beloved over to the drinks stand and both of them took a little glass. But she had been so spoiled for wine over the past decades that she could barely manage a sip of the local tipple. Achim concurred.

'It tastes like it's been made with antifreeze,' he said.

'I fear antifreeze would be more palatable than this

rot', joked Angela. Achim began to laugh loudly, which he only ever did when he'd drunk alcohol. He sounded like an asthmatic sea lion.

'Is he feeling alright?' asked a Harlequin waiter.

'He's just laughing.'

'Okay… Perhaps you'd like to try the punch instead? There's just enough for one last glass.' The waiter gestured towards a bowl, where a single, sad slice of pineapple floated in what remained of the light-brown liquid.

Privately Angela considered it very unlikely that the punch would taste any better than the wine, but she didn't want to seem rude. 'What's in it?' she asked.

'Well, there's some Baugenwitz wine…'

Not a good start, thought Angela.

'Not a good start,' said Achim.

It was lovely that they were still on the same wavelength after all these years! How could she even consider putting this charmed marriage under strain by breaking her pact with her wonderful husband and escaping back to Berlin?

'And on top of that,' continued the Harlequin, 'there's hot eggnog, hot amaretto, hot caramel vodka – and pineapple to be healthy.'

'All of that just to hide the taste of the wine?' asked Angela.

Achim laughed again, gasping for breath and briefly unnerving the Harlequin once more as he ladled the last of the punch into a glass. 'The last glass brings luck!' he announced.

'Please! Allow me!' Achim said with a gallant I-would-die-for-you gesture. He took a sip and shuddered. 'Old Balduin's wife didn't need to bother with hemlock with barrels of this stuff in the cellar.'

'I'll have to throw it away now,' the waiter said irritably as Achim handed him back the almost-full glass. 'You've already drunk from it!'

As the man walked off in a huff, Angela looked around. She wondered what their host was up to. The knight in less-than-shining armour was nowhere to be seen. Many guests had already made their way home, but a few last revellers were still singing drunkenly along to old folk songs. The fruit-seller had taken down the stand and was rolling up her banner. It wasn't just the baron who was missing; his wife hadn't shown her face since the speech either. The girl with the blue hair, on the other hand, was rolling a joint by the fountain. The young policewoman was keeping an impatient eye on the time, no doubt keen to clock off. Mike was trying and comically failing not to stare in her direction.

Katharina von Baugenwitz stepped onto the podium. Signalling to the musicians to stop playing, she announced into the microphone: 'Ladies and gentlemen, all good things must come to an end. We're delighted you turned up in such numbers and are already looking forward to welcoming you at our annual harvest festival this autumn.'

The remaining guests applauded. As she clapped, Angela wondered why the baron had passed up this opportunity to appear in front of an audience. She didn't know him well, but it seemed somewhat out of character to leave the ceremonial farewell to his ex-wife.

'Shall we go?' said Achim, interrupting her thoughts.

'Yes, Muffin, let's go.'

'*Muffin*,' echoed the Harlequin with a smirk.

Achim and Angela ignored him. As they were gesturing to Mike that it was time to leave, Lena the policewoman suddenly hurried past without so much as a glance. Strange, thought Angela. Only an hour ago she'd been so friendly.

Katharina von Baugenwitz approached. 'Are you leaving already?' she said. 'I was hoping to show you around the castle.'

'Perhaps another time,' said Angela. She had no desire to listen to the woman's requests for favours.

'We have a truly magnificent wine cellar.'

'We've already tried the local plonk,' said Achim, making no attempt to conceal his horror at the prospect of having to drink more of it.

'Oh, not that filthy stuff my ex-husband produces. We've got the best wine cellar in eastern Germany. There are Riojas from 1917, clarets from 1929, a 1943 Cheval Blanc.'

Achim was taken aback. 'Wow... those really are the the best years! For wine I mean. They weren't so great for humanity.'

'Are you sure you wouldn't like to sample one or two of these rare vintages?'

'I suppose it might wash the rather nasty taste from my mouth.'

'And the rather nasty memory of the Baugenwitz punch from your mind,' joked Angela.

Achim burst into his sea lion laugh again. Katharina gave a violent start, but quickly pulled herself together. 'Excellent!' she said. 'Shall we make our way to the dungeon?'

'The dungeon?' said Angela.

'Balduin – the one who built this castle – used to keep prisoners there. They say nobody ever came out alive. Now we just use the space for wine of course.'

Angela and Achim followed Katharina into the castle, with Mike a few paces behind them.

The entrance hall was full of paintings of the last few centuries' worth of Baugenwitzes: hunting, banqueting, or just staring crossly at the painter (no doubt wondering how much longer they'd have to stay still). To judge by their expressions, the male members of the family didn't suffer from a lack of self-confidence. Two of them looked especially unpleasant.

'That must be Balduin,' said Angela in front of a seventeenth-century painting showing a knight grinning dementedly as he stood atop a pile of corpses.

'He makes Vlad the Impaler seem like quite a level-headed chap,' said Achim.

'You can see why his wife might have wanted to poison him,' said Angela.

'None of the barons was exactly a paragon of virtue,' said Katharina pointedly. It was clear to Angela that she lumped her ex-husband in with the rest of them.

Angela's gaze fell on a portrait of a man in a suit of the kind the chancellors of the Weimar Republic used to wear. He was sitting at his desk, no doubt attending to

40

some highly important paperwork: perhaps that month's rota for impalings.

'That's Ferdinand, Philipp's great-grandfather. He was a very powerful man in politics and society. His influence went beyond Brandenburg – as far as Berlin. He was far more impressive than our Philipp.'

That's not hard, Angela thought to herself as she pictured the conceited clown in armour.

Obviously she didn't say this out loud.

'That's not hard,' said Achim out loud.

'No, it isn't,' said their guide. If Katharina still harboured any love for her ex-husband, it manifested itself in contempt.

'What a horrible picture!' Achim said in front of painting of a man in a blue aristocrat's outfit and eighteenth-century wig. He was lying in the grass, his face bloody and mutilated, while another man clad in red and yellow was bent over him holding a musket.

'That's putting it lightly,' said Mike, turning pale. The bodyguard had strong muscles but a very weak stomach.

'It's Walter von Baugenwitz,' explained Katharina. 'He lost a duel with Bernhard von Sassen and died an agonising death over the course of a fortnight.'

'What was the reason for the duel?' asked Achim.

'Bernhard insulted Walter by telling him he ran like a duck. He even did an impression, waddling around in front of Walter – who then demanded satisfaction.'

Achim shook his head. 'So he died of a large ego.'

Not a cause of death women were prone to, Angela found herself thinking.

'Come on, let's find the wine,' said Katharina, leading the guests across the hall. Angela noticed that many of the picture frames were damaged. The carpets they were walking on were threadbare and a glance up to the ceiling revealed that the plasterwork was crumbling in places. The castle's interior was mouldering like an aging diva.

Katharina took them down a corridor past a bust of General Hindenburg. Angela could well imagine the circles Philipp's grandfather had moved in during the 1930s. Alongside the general were three glass cabinets: the first contained a morning star, the second a crossbow and the third a musket.

'Is that the gun Walter used in the duel?' asked Angela.

'Yes,' said Katharina without stopping.

Angela saw that the glass above the musket was slightly askew. She had an urge to put it back in place – as a scientist she knew that the gun's metal would oxidise if the cabinet wasn't sealed – but she restrained herself. It was impolite to tidy up in other people's houses.

They turned into a narrower side corridor that led to a heavy wooden door with a wrought-iron handle. Stretched out on a chaise longue in front of the door, Alexa was snoring noisily.

'She snores almost as loudly as you do,' Achim murmured affectionately to his wife. Not for the first time that evening, Mike snorted in amusement.

As Angela weighed up which of the two she should glare at first, Katharina said, 'Ignore her.'

'That would be easier if I had my earplugs with me, but I left them on the bedside table,' said Achim.

Mike made another noise that betrayed amusement.

Angela sighed. In Berlin her bodyguards had had far less insight into her private life. Sometimes it was hard not to long for those days again.

She stepped with the others past the snoring woman, through the heavy wooden door and onto a narrow stone staircase that descended into the catacombs.

Ignoring the electric light switch, Katharina von Baugenwitz took a medieval wooden torch from its mount and lit it. 'This is more appropriate.'

At the bottom of the stairs was a low, vaulted corridor, leading to another wooden door even more solid than the one at the top of the stairs.

'*Voilà* – our wine cellar!' Katharina pressed down the handle but the door wouldn't open. 'Strange…'

'What's strange?' Angela asked.

'The door's locked. It's never locked!'

Angela was surprised by the woman's sudden panic.

'A key might help,' said Achim, stating the obvious.

'There is only one key! Philipp has it – but he never uses it! We always leave the door open, always! Something's wrong!' She pressed the handle down again. And again.

'Do you know what the definition of madness is?' said Achim. 'It's when you keep doing the same thing hoping for a different result.'

'Not now, Muffin,' said Angela. She laid a hand on Katharina's shoulder, but the panic-stricken woman shoved it violently away.

'WHOAH!' Mike leapt in to protect his charge, but

only knocked his head against the vaulted ceiling. 'Ow! *Scheisse!*'

Angela moved to de-escalate the situation. 'Let's all calm down. Mike, would you be so kind as to open the door for us?'

Mike yanked the handle, which came off in his hand. The door remained closed.

'Perhaps you need to try something a little more extreme,' said Angela.

'You mean force it open?' Mike's expression brightened. 'Or shoot the lock?'

'I think forcing it open would be just fine,' said Angela hastily.

Mike took a few steps back then launched himself at the door. There was an almighty sound of splintering wood and the lock gave way. Cursing under his breath, the bodyguard clutched his shoulder.

Katharina pushed open the door and immediately let out a scream. Mike pulled out his gun. Achim assumed the karate basic position. He'd made it as far as green belt in the 1990s, before realising that not only was jogging better for the cardiovascular system, it also meant you got fewer bare feet in your face. Angela, on the other hand, kept her composure. She swiftly took the torch from Katharina and shone it into the cellar.

Amongst the wine barrels and racks full of dusty bottles, Philipp sat motionless, his torso slumped over a huge oak desk.

'NOBODY MOVE!' Mike shouted, moving towards the man in armour, his pistol at the ready. He lifted the baron's head and peered through the open visor. 'He's as dead as a doornail.'

Katharina gave a shriek and began to sob. Angela gestured to her husband. Achim gallantly took her hand and led her out of the vault.

While Mike performed a reconnoitre, finger on the trigger, Angela pressed a switch and the former dungeon flooded with light. Slotting the torch into an empty bracket on the wall, she approached the body. Up to then she'd only come across violent death indirectly in statistics and reports, and she was surprised at how calm she felt. On the desk in front of the body stood a medieval chalice, almost half full. Angela took a closer look.

'Don't touch anything,' said Mike, returning the pistol to its holster. He had satisfied himself that no dangers were lurking in the musty wine cellar.

'I wouldn't dream of it…' said Angela.

'I'm very glad to hear it,' said Mike.

'… at least not without gloves,' she continued, pulling a pair of leather ones from her bag.

'Definitely not a good idea,' said Mike, but he knew his boss well enough by now to realise that there was no point trying to stop her.

Angela put on the gloves and picked up the chalice.

'It looks like the Holy Grail in *Indiana Jones and the Last Crusade*,' said Mike.

As she inspected the ancient vessel, Angela's pulse quickened. 'There are bits of residue inside,' she said. 'It appears the baron was poisoned.' She felt the familiar surge of adrenaline that flowed through her veins whenever she was confronted with an unexpected and complicated task. She'd never expected to experience this again in retirement. Yet now she was! Morally suspect though it might be, Angela had to admit she felt extremely excited about this apparent murder case. More excited than about anything else that had happened in Klein-Freudenstadt so far, even her dance with Achim.

'It could be cork,' said Mike.

'I don't think so. He would have noticed the cork while the wine was being poured.'

'He wouldn't have noticed poison?'

'It could have been slipped into the glass after the wine. And given how much we've all heard about hemlock today, I wouldn't be at all surprised if that is what's in the chalice.'

'Hold on a minute,' said Mike. 'He can't have been murdered.'

'Why not?'

'Look – the door was locked from the inside. How could the killer have made his exit?'

Angela was pondering this when she spotted a broken inkpot on the floor. It looked as if it had been knocked off the desk by the baron in his death throes. Not far from it lay a quill, the nib still wet with ink.

'Mike, could you lift his upper body off the desk.'

'You do realise we ought to leave this to the police?'

'Or I could do it myself...'

Mike sighed the sigh of thousands of other officials who'd had to work under Angela over the years. He lifted the baron's torso. On the desk beneath, a scrap of paper was revealed. And scrawled on the paper was:

a

'What does that mean?' asked Mike.

'Well, my dear Mike,' said Angela, fancying that she sounded exactly like Sherlock Holmes. 'I can only assume it's a clue that will lead us to the killer.'

9

'I'm sorry to disagree,' said Mike with a condescending smile that showed he wasn't sorry at all, 'but this was definitely suicide. A strange suicide, yes. But not as strange as a murder' – he pointed at the door again – 'committed with the door locked from the inside and no perpetrator.'

'Let's not rush to any hasty judgments,' said Angela. Over the course of her career she'd learned a number of things. First, that you couldn't be one hundred per cent certain of anything in life. Second, that her hunches were correct 81.4 per cent of the time. (This was according to Achim, who had informed her of the statistic on a day she'd lost three successive votes in the Bundestag. He'd meant to cheer her up but his timing had been hopeless. She'd nearly replied that she found 81.4 per cent of his qualities endearing, and maybe he ought to work out whether or not his penchant for making such calculations was one of these.) And third, when a man gave her a condescending smile, it was usually a sign she was onto something. If she had a euro for each patronising male smile, she sometimes thought, she would be able to finance the clean energy revolution single-handedly.

So Angela trusted her instinct and ignored this smile as she had all the others in the past. She hoped this was one of the 81.4 per cent of occasions on which she was right. After all, a murder victim who'd scribbled a clue just before he died was far more exciting than a mere suicide, however dramatic.

Angela removed the gloves and began to nose around the wine cellar for further clues. The bottles in the racks were ordered by date. The more recent vintages had the years marked on the labels, while the age of the older ones had to be inferred from the ever-thicker layers of dust on the bottles. At the far end of the cellar was a huge wine barrel. A perfect hiding place for a killer! she thought, then couldn't help smiling at herself. She'd never entertained such crazy thoughts in her life. It was thrilling!

Angela knocked on the barrel. It didn't sound hollow, as she'd hoped, and for a moment she pictured a person, with flippers, goggles and oxygen tank, hiding in the wine. No, that was too far-fetched. She mustn't get carried away by her fantasies – as she had in 2015, when for a few weeks she'd believed the Germans would actually welcome refugees into the country with open arms.

She made her way around the barrel and examined the wall behind. Was there a secret door, perhaps? Leading to a passage, down which the murderer could have fled?

In the dim light she could only make out the large arch bricks, but no door. Not even a lever or a button to open up a secret passage, like the one in the White House used by so many presidents to smuggle their lovers in and out. Or by Barack Obama to smuggle in and out the cigarettes he had to hide from Michelle.

'It's time we went back up,' called Mike. 'The police will be here soon and they'll want you to make a statement. You ought to be gone before the press appear.'

Up to now Angela hadn't been worried about the press. There wasn't a single journalist living in Klein-Freudenstadt. Sooner or later, though, a local hack from the *Uckermarker Herald* was bound to turn up from nearby Templin and make a name for themselves with the headline EX-CHANCELLOR FINDS BODY. Whereupon the national media would descend for weeks. Her peace and quiet would come to an abrupt end.

Besides, Angela knew there was no way the police investigators would let her play the amateur sleuth. For a moment this made her feel sad, but she pulled herself together. Expert work should be left to the experts. And let's face it, she was about as much of a genuine detective as Melania Trump was a genuine feminist.

As she passed the wine barrel on the way out, something flitted by on the ground. A white mouse! Not being one of those women who was irrationally frightened of mice, she didn't scream. Instead she analysed the path it took. The mouse hadn't come from the direction of the broken door, so it must have been in the cellar for a while. Was there a secret passage after all? She was about to turn back to investigate where the mouse was heading when she heard Achim shout, 'I need your help!'

49

'What's the matter?' called Angela.

'I don't know whether I should wake up the dead man's wife or not.'

The wife!

Was she still asleep?

Or just pretending?

It was time to find out. Surely it couldn't hurt to collect a few more clues to hand over to the experts from the police?

10

'She's snoring like a world champion,' said Angela. Alexa von Baugenwitz was still lying on the chaise longue. She was like a sailor who'd helped himself generously from the rum barrel after crossing the equator, then fallen into it and spent the night there.

'Strictly speaking, like the runner-up,' said Achim. 'You're the champion.'

'ACHIM!'

'Yes?'

'I do love you, but sometimes I'd like to—'

'Scold me for my loose tongue?'

Angela had been about to say something stronger, but she let it go. She looked at Mike. He was trying and failing to console Katharina von Baugenwitz. Seemingly unaware of his presence, she was just staring torpidly at the floor.

Angela remembered Katharina's sudden alarm when the door wouldn't open. It was strange, as if somehow she'd known that the baron was in danger. Could she have an inkling as to the identity of the killer – assuming it really was murder?

She decided not to broach the matter. Not only would it be disrespectful to question her while she was in shock, it was also unnecessary. Naturally the woman would tell the detective inspector everything. Unless, that is, she was the killer herself…

'Should we wake up the baroness now?' said Achim, interrupting her thoughts.

'Yes, I think we should.'

'But how? I mean, we know she takes sleeping pills. I've tried everything, even shaking her.'

Angela looked at the baroness. She stank of booze and seemed to be asleep. But then she was a professional actress – all this could be a sham. If it had been murder, Alexa had been close to the scene of the crime and thus was a prime suspect. Maybe she'd been about to make her escape when she heard Angela and the others heading for the wine cellar and, in a panic, thought her only option was to lie on the chaise longue and pretend to be sleeping off her drunkenness. Well, the time had come to find out!

'I've got an idea,' said Angela.

'Fall asleep yourself and hope your snoring wakes her up?' said Achim.

Angela ignored this suggestion. 'We'll stab her with my brooch pin,' she said loudly in the sleeping woman's direction. From her red blazer she removed the beautiful gold-leaf brooch, which she'd bought many years ago with her first ever minister's salary, and approached the baroness.

51

The woman kept snoring. Either she really was in a deep sleep or she was determined not to blow her cover. 'I think stabbing her in the cheek would work best,' said Angela.

The snoring continued unabated.

'I just hope I don't slip and stab her *in the eye* by accident,' continued Angela, doubling down on the charade.

The baroness snored even louder. Either Angela's hunch was wrong or the snoring meant: I'm not going to let you intimidate me!

The pin was just millimetres from Alexa von Baugenwitz's cheek and Angela was feeling almost woozy from the alcoholic fumes coming from the woman's mouth. She'd been bluffing, but now she had to make a decision. To stab or not to stab?

'Stick it in,' said a voice. Angela spun around. It was Pia, not looking in the least upset. Did she not yet know that the baron was dead? Or was she just callous?

'It's her fault the old bastard topped himself.'

Okay, callous.

'Pia, please…' said Katharina, who seemed to have emerged from her state of shock and had started to shake.

'Neither of them gave a shit how they treated you!'

Aha! Was an ugly back-story about to come to light?

'Please!' Katharina began to shake even more.

'Okay, okay.' Pia said. She sat down cross-legged on the floor and took out her phone. Whatever was on the screen was clearly more important than the death of her ex-stepfather.

'She—' Katharina tried to find the words to explain

Pia's behaviour. 'You do everything for them... and then...' Tears flooded her eyes again.

Angela felt sorry for the woman. Of all the people in the castle she was the one who'd reacted most normally. As delicately as she could, Angela asked, 'You suspected something when the door wouldn't open, didn't you?'

Katharina, who'd had barely any colour in her cheeks before, now turned completely ashen and struggled to speak: 'Philipp... he... he wanted to take his life because we've got... such large debts here. He was so ashamed.'

Angela hadn't had the impression that the baron was a man who felt shame. But she could hardly say this to Katharina von Baugenwitz, who was weeping again. If it really had been suicide it would be unseemly to drill her with more questions.

'The cops are here. Hooray,' said blue-haired Pia. She sounded about as enthusiastic as Barack Obama had when Angela asked him if he too had had the pleasure of attending an opera during his visit to Beijing.

The policewoman who'd made such an impression on Mike entered the corridor, accompanied by a short, tubby man in his early sixties whose few hairs lay in a random fashion on his head. Curiously, he looked both as if he'd just got out of bed and as if he always looked that way. Because he wore a crumpled suit rather than police uniform, Angela surmised that he must be the detective inspector.

Since Lena's entrance Mike had been edging nervously backwards. Now she gave him a nod, which sent him back another half-step into a stand with a vase that

53

toppled over. Before it shattered on the stone floor it was deftly caught by Achim.

'I'm astounded at myself,' said Achim as Mike stammered his thanks.

'You can lead a horse to water,' said the teenage girl cryptically, without looking up from her screen, 'but he'd rather have a proper drink.'

'I could do with a drink right now,' sighed the inspector, 'but it doesn't agree with my pills. Most of my pills don't even agree with my pills.'

'May I remind you that you're here for a dead body, not for cocktail hour,' said Angela. Men whining about their medicines reminded her of cabinet meetings.

'Yes.' The short, tubby man sighed again. 'Right. So who found the body, then?'

'That was me,' said Angela.

The inspector pictured the looming media furore. 'I hate my life,' he said.

'I'll be out of here before the press arrive.'

'Whatever. I still hate my life.'

Truly the inspector was not the epitome of cheerfulness. 'The body is down in the wine cellar,' said Angela.

'Damp air is bad for my rheumatism.'

Angela subscribed to the idea that everybody was able to do one thing better than everyone else. There was nobody better at conducting than Leonard Bernstein, nobody better at painting than Vincent van Gogh. And probably nobody better at whinging than this man.

'Perhaps you would be so kind as to introduce

yourself?' said Achim. He couldn't abide bad manners, especially when they were directed towards his wife.

'Hannemann – Hartmut Hannemann,' said the inspector in a kind of extreme lacklustre parody of James Bond. 'Chief of Klein-Freudenstadt police.'

'Shall we get it over with then?' said Angela.

'Why not,' sighed Hannemann. 'That way in half an hour I can be back in bed, staring at the ceiling and wondering why my wife left me.'

A few possible reasons occurred to Angela, but she kept them to herself.

'I'll come with you,' she said. She wanted to make sure the inspector didn't record the case as suicide without first considering the more exciting alternative!

11

Angela, Hannemann and Lena stood by the desk where the body lay slumped just as they'd found it half an hour earlier, except that the note with the mysterious 'a' was now visible. Mike stayed in the background, eager to avoid further humiliation. Achim was upstairs with the women, sorting out a sedative and a glass of water for Katharina von Baugenwitz.

'Well,' Hannemann said, looking at the chalice, 'if I ever kill myself I can tell you it won't be with poison.'

'How would you do it?' asked Mike.

'I'd go up in a hot-air balloon and jump—'

Angela wished Mike hadn't posed the question.

'—right on top of my ex-wife...'

He seemed to have thought this scenario through in some detail.

'… and if she was with the undertaker I could kill two turds with one stone, so to speak.'

'The undertaker?' Angela was unable to curb her natural curiosity, though she realised her mistake the moment she said it.

'Apparently he's "jollier" than I am.'

'Do you see anything unusual about the body?' she said, trying to direct him back to the matter in hand.

'If I flattened them it would stop her posting on Facebook about how happy they are.'

'Did you hear what I said?'

'They made risotto. I had to look up what that is.'

'Please!'

'It's just rice. Bog-standard rice!'

'I don't believe it was a suicide,' said Angela, getting to the point.

'What makes you think that?' The inspector reluctantly returned to the here and now.

'Look at the piece of paper.'

'What about it?' Hannemann picked it up, but from the clueless expression on his face she could see that his grey cells weren't firing on all cylinders. If they had any cylinders in the first place.

'It's a clue.'

'To what?'

'To the identity of killer.'

'What killer?'

'I told you I think it was a murder.'

'What makes you think that?'

'The piece of paper!'

'What about it?'

Angela sensed that the conversation was going around in circles. She felt anger welling up inside her, but she didn't want to vent it. She didn't want to be the arrogant ex-chancellor, but the concerned citizen of Klein-Freudenstadt. Perhaps Lena would understand. She tried to catch the policewoman's eye.

'The cellar was locked from the inside,' said Lena. 'There's no way somebody else could have killed him.'

'That's exactly what I said!' Mike beamed, delighted to find himself on the same wavelength. Lena gave him a curt nod and didn't smile back.

'Maybe there's a secret passage,' said Angela. The expressions of the two police officers made her feel faintly silly. Was she being ridiculous?

'While running the check for the insurance company I examined the old plans of the castle. There is no secret passage,' said Lena.

Angela was starting to feel even sillier, but she stuck to her guns: 'I don't think a secret passage would be marked on any plans.'

'Have you actually discovered one?' asked Hannemann.

'No,' said Angela. She held the man's gaze and made a diamond shape with her hands. As always, it helped to ground her.

'So why are we discussing this?'

'You need to look at things from every angle.'

'Who's the expert here? You or me?'

By now Angela had serious doubts that Hannemann could be classed as an expert.

'Shouldn't we at least look for a secret passage?'

'I will tell you what we're going to do. We're going to have the body taken away. Then we're going to do a post-mortem, as is only proper. Then we're going to close the case. And then we're going to take a day off to make up for the overtime tonight.'

Angela realised she wasn't going to be able to change the inspector's mind. Lena didn't seem particularly keen to take a closer look at the piece of paper either. Instead she was nibbling away nervously at a fingernail. Could she be intimidated by her boss? No, that wasn't it – she'd already looked a bit weird when she left the festival. But why…?

Angela told herself to snap out of it. To suspect a policewoman of a crime that might not have even taken place was taking this detective game too far. All the same, she wasn't ready to just give up yet. She didn't have the slightest confidence in Hannemann's ability to solve a murder. Besides, she hadn't felt so much enjoyment and energy in weeks. She decided to try a different tactic: 'I'd like to attend the post-mortem.'

There was a stunned silence.

Before anyone had time to object, Angela went on: 'I've only ever seen them on television before.'

'Absolutely no way!' said the inspector.

'In that case I think I'll stay here until the press arrive,' said Angela.

Hannemann blanched.

'I can deal with the media,' Angela went on, with a hint of sadism. 'Can you?'

It was clear that the prospect was as distressing for Hannemann as his ex-wife's risotto photograph.

'Okay, okay, you can come along tomorrow.'

Angela gave an impish smile.

'And now I hate my life even more,' said Hannemann, putting the piece of paper in his pocket. Lena followed him out of the cellar. And at a safe distance, Mike followed Lena. Angela stayed a while longer, contemplating the 'a'. Was it the first letter of a name? Alexa von Baugenwitz, for example? But in that case wouldn't it have been capitalised?

Making the diamond shape with her hands again, Angela engaged her scientist's brain. Before I can form a preliminary hypothesis, she thought, I must collect more information.

12

Angela lay wide awake beside Achim, who was out for the count. As in the first couple of weeks in her new home, she couldn't get to sleep. At that time she'd lain awake mulling over political problems for which she was no longer responsible. It was only after about a fortnight that she'd more or less grown used to the idea that she no longer had to solve the world's crises. But then she found she couldn't sleep because it was so damn quiet! There was no city noise, no police sirens, no drunken revellers. How could anyone sleep in such conditions? Finally, though, she did get used to the quiet – even to the owl, which was the only thing that ever made a sound at night. Yet here she was, lying wide awake again. And all because there was another problem. One she might be able to solve!

As she reached for the pen and pad she always kept on her bedside table, she tugged the duvet, exposing Achim's feet. Her husband slept like a baby – except when his toes felt a draught. His right big toe was particularly sensitive, capable of predicting changes in the weather more accurately than most metereologists.

'Why are you awake?' said Achim, removing his earplugs.

'I believe the baron was murdered,' said Angela. It was the first time she had broached this theory in her husband's presence.

Achim sat up. Unlike the others he didn't dismiss her theory. After all, he knew that Angela was correct in 81.4 per cent of cases. His basic position, therefore, was that it was safer to trust her intuition.

Angela drew an 'a' on the pad and showed it to her husband. 'The victim wrote this on a scrap of paper just before he died. What could it mean?'

'Hmmm...' said Achim, as he always did when he was thinking.

Angela waited.

'Hmmm...'

It dawned on Angela that she wasn't going to get anything more substantial out of him.

'There is something I can tell you...' he said.

'What?'

'I'm pretty sure it's going to rain tomorrow afternoon. I can feel it in my toe.'

'So you have no idea what the letter means?'

'I'm sorry, Muffinella.'

Achim called his wife Muffinella when he felt he'd let her down. He needn't have worried. In twenty-five years of marriage Angela had never felt let down by her husband. Irritated, frustrated and annoyed, yes. But let down? She just couldn't imagine this wonderful man letting her down.

'Maybe we'll learn more at the post-mortem,' she said.

'Post-mortem?'

'We're going to watch the body being cut open tomorrow,' she said with a smile.

'What a delightful prospect.'

'It's something different.'

'So we're playing detectives?' Achim had started to smile too.

'Sherlock Holmes and Doctor Watson.'

'I have no doubt that you will make an excellent Watson. You may write a book about my deductions.'

'If anyone's Sherlock here, it's me!'

'I think you'll find,' Achim grinned, 'that I am a quantum chemist, whereas you're just a simple physicist.'

Angela picked up a pillow and whacked him affectionately on the head. They both laughed. The commotion woke Putin, who was dozing at the foot of the bed. The pug leapt up, causing the couple to laugh even more at his futile attempts to hop onto the bed, until Angela said, 'Come on, mouse, let me help you.'

She lifted Putin onto the duvet, whereupon he immediately calmed down.

'I deduce that creature is not a mouse, Doctor Watson,' said Achim, posing with an imaginary pipe.

'I am flabbergasted! How the devil did you work that out? You really are an outstanding detective, Sherlock.'

Angela was happy to humour her husband, being well aware who would actually be leading the investigation.

'How about we're both Sherlock?' Achim suggested. 'We could be Sherlock and Sherlockella!'

Angela grinned. No matter what they called each other, they had one thing in common with Arthur Conan Doyle's famous figures: she and Achim were the best companions imaginable!

13

The post-mortem wasn't in Klein-Freudenstadt. Naturally the village didn't have its own pathology department, just a doctor and a dentist on the verge of retirement who only worked half days. In an emergency people could reach him in the afternoons on a golf course forty kilometres away, though he never listened to his voicemail until the eighteenth green.

Angela, Achim and Mike drove to the hospital in Templin in the car that had been put at her disposal as an ex-chancellor. Angela had chosen the model herself: the cheapest and smallest electric car on the market. When they arrived, she was the first to get out. She had disguised herself in a long black wig and 1970s sunglasses, although the black trousers, orange–red blazer and matching orange–red Longchamp handbag were something of a give-away.

Putin was home alone, which meant they had to be back within a couple of hours. Otherwise the pug would punish them with a deposit on the carpet at the foot of the bed. In his own way, Angela sometimes thought, this Putin was a liability too.

As he walked behind her, Achim remarked that Angela in her disguise looked like Gina Lollobrigida. His comment bore zero semblance to reality but she was flattered anyway. Achim hadn't bothered to conceal his identity. Why should anyone recognise him now, seeing as virtually no one had known of his existence during all her years as chancellor? There had been that memorable incident at the G7 summit when they wouldn't let him into the dinner at the conference hotel. When he protested that he was Angela Merkel's husband, one of the security guards had said, 'Yeah, right, and I'm Romano Prodi's gay lover.' Achim had found a bench in a nearby park, basked in the evening sun and tucked into a delicious schnitzel sandwich. It had been a much more enjoyable evening than he'd expected.

The last to climb out of the car was Mike. He still hadn't got used to the 'sardine tin', as he privately called it. The three of them made their way to the rear entrance of the hospital, where Inspector Hannemann was waiting for them. He didn't exactly look thrilled at seeing Angela again. Mike was disappointed to see that Lena hadn't come.

'Let's get this over with,' said Hannemann.

'Good morning to you, too,' said Achim, outraged

at the man's lack of respect for his beloved wife. Ignoring him, Hannemann opened the door and led them all downstairs. Angela took off the wig and sunglasses, stashed them in a large bag and breathed in the sterile tang of the hospital. It vaguely reminded her of Pope Benedict's aftershave.

The examination room in the basement was straight out of a TV crime series: neon light, huge drawers that presumably contained the corpses, and a few dissection tables, only one of which was currently in use. Beside it stood an elderly lady in a white coat, her substantial girth obscuring the view of the corpse. It was clear, however, that the dead body belonged to the baron since various pieces of armour were lying on a side table.

'Doctor Radszinski,' said Hannemann, greeting the pathologist. Until now Angela had thought that it was only thin women who looked haggard, but Radszinski proved the opposite. A life spent cutting open bodies evidently took its toll on the complexion.

'Hannemann,' replied the pathologist. To judge from her voice the woman subsisted on alcohol, cigarettes and sandpaper. She gave him a hostile glance. 'Shouldn't you still be on sick leave? You look like shit.'

'And you still look like Gary Oldman.'

Angela performed an intervention. 'Have you completed the post-mortem?'

'I've just opened him up,' Radszinski, moving to allow them a view of the corpse.

'Next I'll remove the organs – starting with the spleen.' She placed the wobbly body part on a metal tray.

Mike emitted an indeterminate sound. He had turned very white.

'Now the liver… and the heart.'

White shaded into green.

'Would you like to wait outside?' Angela asked Mike.

'No, no… I'm fine,' said Mike. He was a bodyguard after all, not a ballerina! But when Radszinski began to pull out the baron's six-metre-long intestine, his legs started to give way. He clapped a hand in front of his mouth.

'If he pukes on the stiff—' growled the pathologist.

'Muffin?' Angela said.

'Yes?'

'Please take Mike outside.'

'But he said he was fine.'

'Does he look fine?'

'Not particularly.'

'What if he passes out? Or needs to vomit?'

'I'll take him out.'

As Achim led the bodyguard away, Dr Radszinski slapped the intestine noisily on top of the other organs.

'Is removing the organs really necessary for the investigation?' asked Angela.

'No,' said the pathologist. 'I just like watching men who think they're hard go to pieces.'

Angela knew she ought to disapprove, but she could empathise. She got a bit of a thrill herself at the sight of macho types losing their nerve. 'So what has your examination revealed?' she asked.

'The man swallowed hemlock.'

'Just as I suspected!' Angela said in delight, before

trying belatedly to hide her pleasure behind a serious expression.

'Don't forget – it wasn't murder,' said Hannemann.

Angela ignored him. 'Is it possible he didn't notice the taste of the poison?'

'Well, at first hemlock does taste sweet… But given the degree to which it was diluted by the wine, he would have had to take at least three swigs.'

'But it could be undetectable in a sweetish wine?'

'Perhaps to begin with, but the aftertaste is sharp. He would certainly have noticed that – even if he was knocking it back.'

'A killer,' said Hannemann triumphantly, 'would have chosen a poison with no taste whatsoever.'

'Not if they wanted to make a clever allusion to the baron's ancestor Balduin, who was also poisoned with hemlock in the seventeenth century,' said Angela.

'Who would have guessed that you of all people would have such a vivid imagination,' sneered the inspector.

This Hannemann was a waste of space, Angela decided. She'd sooner trust Mike to perform a kidney transplant than the policeman to lead a murder investigation. She turned to the pathologist, 'Is there anything else unusual about the body?'

'You mean apart from the fact that he's got a tattoo declaring his eternal love for Katharina von Baugenwitz?'

'His ex-wife?'

'Yes. Do you want to see it? It's on his left buttock.'

'No, thank you.'

'There was also something a bit odd about his armour.

There's a strange protuberance in the right gauntlet... Come on, I'll show you.'

The pathologist went over to the table with the bits of armour and pointed to the gauntlet. Now Angela saw it too: the palm had a metal attachment fused to it. It was in the form of a hexagram.

'Maybe some sort of satanic thing,' said Radszinski.

It was a possibility, thought Angela, but she was more inclined towards a different explanation. To her the protrusion looked like a kind of key. To open a door to a secret passage, for example. A door through which a murderer could escape. But then the gauntlet wouldn't have been found on the corpse's hand... Unless of course the culprit had run back after opening the door and put the gauntlet back on the baron to conceal the existence of the secret passage!

Angela was in a state of high excitement. The hexagram could be the key not only to a secret passage, but to solving the murder. But to find out whether she was right or if this was one of the 18.6 per cent of cases when she was wrong, she would have to pilfer the gauntlet from the examination room.

The inspector wouldn't be a problem, but outsmarting the pathologist might be trickier.

She turned to Hannemann, arranging her face into a picture of feminine meekness. 'I think,' she purred in a voice she had honed to perfection over decades of dealing with wannabe alpha males, 'that you are quite right. After all, you're the expert. I just got carried away.'

Hannemann stared at her in amazement. He could

hardly believe his ears: no woman had paid him a compliment since about 1995, and even then she'd quickly taken it back. 'You're admitting I know better?'

'Yes. I admit that you know better.' If the situation demanded, Angela could swallow her pride.

'So you're saying that you don't have my expertise.'

'That's right. I'm saying that I don't have your expertise.'

'So I'm cleverer than you.'

'Don't push it.'

'Fair enough... Does that mean we can go now?' asked Hannemann.

'I'd just like to stay here a while longer and chat to Dr Radszinski about her work,' said Angela. 'But I'll manage on my own. You go ahead – you've earned a break.'

'You can say that again.' The inspector departed the examination room without another word.

'It's good that you stayed,' said Radszinksi. 'I could do with a hand clearing away the organs. Could you shove the intestine in the freezer back there?'

Angela's brain was whirring. Not only because she was eager to avoid touching the baron's viscera, but because she had to find a way to distract the pathologist while she pilfered the gauntlet. She had never imagined that retirement would be so stimulating! As she looked at the fat doctor, she remembered a trick the other ministers occasionally used to play on her trusted ally Peter Altmaier. It was a little cruel, but this was a murder investigation after all. The situation justified it.

'You've got something on your shoe,' she said.

'What?' Radszinski tried to examine her shoes and

failed as miserably as Peter Altmaier always had when this trick was played on him.

'It looks like part of the baron's appendix,' said Angela. 'Why don't you take a look in the mirror?'

As Radszinski trundled to the other end of the room, Angela acted fast. She grabbed the gauntlet and dropped it into her bag. Now she needed to make herself scarce.

'There's nothing on my shoe,' said Radszinski from the mirror.

'It must've been a trick of the light.' Angela was already at the door, grasping the handle.

'Hey! I thought you were going to help me!'

'I've just remembered that I have another set of intestines to attend to.'

'Oh, really?' The doctor sounded surprised.

'Yes – Putin's.'

Angela hurried up the stairs while Radszinski stared after her. It was the first time in her life the ex-chancellor had stolen anything, but she didn't feel particularly disturbed or even thrilled. It was more a case of surprise, similar to what she'd felt as a physicist when an experiment delivered unexpected results. Only this time the subject of the experiment was herself: Angela Merkel, pensioner, thief… and detective!

14

When Angela and Achim arrived home, they found Putin sitting proudly on the bedroom rug beside his latest creation. Angela gathered him up in her arms. 'We should never have left you on your own for so long, should we, my little mouse?' she cooed.

'He isn't a mouse,' said Achim, picking up the mess with a plastic bag and privately regretting their purchase of a shaggy Greek flokati rug.

'He doesn't know that though.'

'He'll develop an identity disorder.'

'Or turn into a pugmouse,' grinned Angela. 'Throw the rug onto the terrace and we'll clean it later. First we're going to the castle.'

'Why?'

'I've uncovered a clue, Sherlock.'

'Well, Sherlockella, that certainly does arouse my curiosity. But I'm afraid we can't go to the castle right now.'

'Why? Because of the rug?'

'No, because Mike must accompany you on all excursions. And he is in no state to do that at the moment.'

It was true. Mike had spent the entire journey home on the back seat, his large head stuck out of the window to let fresh air waft around his ashen-white nostrils. Now he was lying on his sofa bed in the summer house that had been converted into an apartment.

'Let's go and see how he is,' said Angela, putting Putin down and pushing open the glass door that led directly from the bedroom into the dreamy garden lined with rhododendrons.

'And besides,' said Achim. 'We've got an appointment with the tour guide – remember?'

Angela sighed. This was what happened when your calendar had been managed by a PA for decades. Despite her eagerness to find a secret door that could be opened with the gauntlet, Angela knew she couldn't stand up Marie. That would be unacceptably rude. And she really was keen to learn more about Klein-Freudenstadt – as well as to find out what was weighing the woman down. Perhaps she'd be able to help her.

'Okay, first let me check on Mike.' Angela went out into the garden and breathed in the sweet perfume of the rhododendrons. She walked past Achim's Hobbit garden gnomes: Frodo, Bilbo and Samwise, and a scowling Gollum with a pointed hat upon whom Putin especially liked to urinate.

Angela knocked on the wooden door of the summer house.

'Come in,' came a feeble groan.

Angela was shocked by the mess that greeted her in the small apartment, but only because she was married to a man who was preternaturally tidy. The shoes and clothes lying around, the dirty dishes in the sink and the empty milk carton on the table were hardly out of the ordinary – unlike the pistol hanging in a holster over the chair.

'What can I do for you?' asked Mike, making an effort to sit up on the sofa. His voice quavered faintly.

'I came to pick you up for our tour of the village, but you'd be better off staying here to rest.'

'It's my job to accompany you everywhere,' Mike said, slipping his black socks into his perfectly polished black shoes. When it came to his work attire, the bodyguard was meticulous.

'But if you don't feel well…'

71

'That makes no difference. It's my duty to protect you. And my pleasure.'

'Your pleasure?'

'It is a pleasure to do my duty.'

Angela could relate to this; she felt the same. And yet she didn't want to make Mike feel worse. After all it was her fault he was in this sorry state. 'It's fine – stay here. What could possibly happen to me in Klein-Freudenstadt?'

Angela was about to leave the room when she heard Mike say, 'Famous last words.'

The bodyguard was on his feet, looking more serious than she'd seen him ever before. 'You still think that the castle owner was murdered,' he said.

'Perhaps I do… but you are of a different opinion.'

'What I think or believe is irrelevant. In any case it's not for me to say what I think. But I do know that you won't give up.'

It was true. Giving up was not one of Angela's strong points.

'Let's just assume there really is a killer. That inspector is hardly likely to find him,' he continued.

Angela could hardly disagree with this.

'And that being the case, who is the only danger to the killer?' The colour had returned to Mike's cheeks; he looked and sounded authoritative.

'Me?'

'Exactly,' Mike said, buckling his holster with the pistol.

At that moment Angela understood that playing detectives was no game.

15

The sun shone down on the market square of Klein-Freudenstadt as if to say, 'How could a murder possibly occur in this idyllic part of the world?' Angela trotted along, carrying her Longchamp bag with the gauntlet inside it. As she passed the fruit stall, she noticed that the banner protesting against the sale of the castle had been fixed to the stand. She stopped. Wasn't the matter closed now that the baron was dead?

'It's even more necessary today,' said her namesake the fruit-seller, as if she could read her thoughts.

'How come?' asked Angela. Out of the corner of her eye she could see Mike scoping the surrounding area even more thoroughly than usual, while Achim strolled across the square with Putin, who was eagerly sniffing out the latest news bulletins left by other local dogs. Achim liked to refer to this as 'canine social media'.

'Because now,' said the fruit-seller, 'Alexa von Baugenwitz will inherit the land we farm. And she will definitely try to sell the whole shebang.'

'How can you be so sure?'

'This place is way too provincial for her. She was always urging Philipp to sell up so they could get themselves somewhere smart in London, Paris or wherever.'

'And yesterday the baron promised in front of the whole village that he wouldn't sell, meaning Alexa would be trapped here forever.' If anyone had a motive to kill Philipp, Angela thought, it was his sole heir. And of course the 'a' could stand for Alexa.

'Philipp only said that to please the crowd,' said the

73

other Angela bitterly. 'He wanted to leave too.'

'Were you and the baron perhaps close once upon a time?' said Angela, feeling another surge of pride. She sounded like a real detective! But her pleasure was short-lived.

'Do you know how much of your business that is?'

'None?'

'To put it mildly.' The woman began angrily sorting fruit that didn't need to be sorted. Angela thought how the 'a' could stand for this Angela too. After all, the woman would lose her livelihood if the castle were sold. On the other hand, if she had killed the baron, she would now have to kill his wife too for the same motive.

At this point a proper investigator would ask something like: 'Where were you at the time of the murder?' However, there were two reasons to refrain from posing this question. First, the killer was hardly going to say: 'Why, thank you for asking! I went down to the wine cellar and poured hemlock into the baron's chalice.' And second, this woman seemed quite aggressive. She might well hurl one of her apples in the ex-chancellor's face.

'Are you going to buy anything or just stand there asking stupid questions?' said the other Angela. She seemed to be growing more and more furious by the moment.

Angela resisted the temptation to say, 'Stand here asking stupid questions,' and instead answered, 'No, I'm not baking today. We've got an appointment with the tour guide.'

'Marie?' said the fruit-seller with a nasty smirk.

'Yes.'

'Oh, but she's going to be very upset today.'

'Why?'

'Well, I'll give you three guesses who the father of her choccy baby is.'

The baron! But Angela quickly put the thought to one side. 'That's a totally unacceptable thing to say, don't you think?' she said. Now it was her turn to feel like hurling fruit in anger. It was astonishing. Only yesterday Angela had thought she could become friends with this woman. How could she have been so wide of the mark? In her career she'd been a good judge of people. In normal life this appeared to be much harder.

'Chocomix? Is that better?' came the mocking reply.

Angela was reaching for an apple – the hardest-looking one she could see – when she heard Mike whisper loudly behind her, 'What a bitch!'

'What did you say?' asked the woman, outraged.

'By all means repeat it,' Angela told Mike. 'I don't mind at all.'

Mike obliged.

Angela gave a malicious smile and turned to walk away.

'I'm glad I never voted for you!' the fruit-seller called out behind her.

'Well I managed perfectly well without your vote,' Angela was tempted to reply. But she knew it would be arrogant. Besides, a disturbing thought had suddenly occurred to her.

If this angry woman really was the murderer, might she not easily get violent with an amateur sleuth?

16

Angela, Achim, Mike and Putin were waiting in the middle of the village square. Achim was humming some 1960s ditty that was beginning to grate on the others' nerves. Even Putin was gearing up to a growl.

'Maybe Marie isn't going to show up,' said Mike. 'I mean, if that bitch is right.'

Achim was on the point of objecting to the body-guard's unchivalrous language when a voice from behind said, 'Sorry I'm late.'

All three turned around. Marie's eyes were swollen. She looked as if she'd been up all night crying, then tried unsuccessfully to hide her distress by caking on the makeup. If the 'bitch' – Angela only allowed herself even to think such words if they were strictly accurate – had been telling the truth rather than spreading a malicious rumour, the young woman must be distraught at the death of the father of her unborn child.

Suddenly the thought popped into Angela's head that Marie might have killed the baron. Perhaps he'd refused to leave his wife Alexa for her? She'd reacted so strangely when asked if she was coming to the festival… Had she already planned the murder?

On the other hand the woman's name was Marie Horstmann, neither of which began with 'a'.

But… hold on… there was an 'a' in Marie…

Nonsense, Angela told herself. Why would the baron begin his message with the second letter of the killer's name? There had been no sign that the first had been rubbed out or removed. Still, to be absolutely sure Angela would have liked another glimpse of the piece of paper, which was presumably now stuffed in one of Inspector Hannemann's drawers, never again to see the light of day. It was annoying that she hadn't taken a picture of it. Not that she had a smartphone – after all those years in government she'd chosen a mobile which couldn't receive WhatsApp messages or emails. A phone you could only telephone with – what a brilliant time- and stress-saving invention! Even if her old Nokia brick didn't allow her to photograph clues.

'Shall we go?' said Marie.

The young woman was clearly trying to put on a brave face. No, her suspicions were nonsense, thought Angela. This was a perfectly normal, friendly woman. It was impossible to imagine her killing the father of her child, no matter how much he'd hurt her.

Throughout her career, Angela had been served well by assuming the worst about people's character when meeting them for the first time. In truth she'd rarely been proved wrong. But in the normal world – even when she was playing detective – this approach was unhelpful.

'Yes, let's go,' Angela said cheerfully, hoping that Marie would return her smile. But the woman didn't appear to be in the mood. Instead she led the group to a large black stone outside the church, which stood out from the smaller grey cobbles.

'This stone,' she said, 'is the so-called *Stone of Tears*. It's dedicated to Adelheid, second wife of Balduin von Baugenwitz. She liberated the people from the tyrant by poisoning him with hemlock…'

And now Alexa von Baugenwitz might have poisoned her husband in exactly the same way! thought Angela.

'… but then – or so one version of the story goes – Adelheid couldn't live with her guilt and so threw herself from the bell tower…'

They all looked up.

'… landing right here.'

They all looked back down.

'That's why the villagers laid the stone of remembrance. This one, on the other hand,' Maria said, pointing to another large stone that was much lighter than other grey ones around it, 'is the *Stone of Shame*. For centuries this is where the inhabitants of Klein-Freudenstadt have shown their contempt for Balduin, who first made his wife a murderer, then a suicide victim.'

'And how do they show their contempt, exactly?' Achim asked.

'By spitting on it?' Angela deduced from the light colouring of the stone.

'Do you want to have a go too?' Marie asked.

They all exchanged glances.

'Don't feel you have to,' the guide said, smiling for the first time. It was a faint smile, but a smile all the same. Hoping to encourage it further, Angela said, 'Alright, then!' and spat on the stone.

'Excellent!' said Marie, now grinning broadly.

Mike and Achim added their expectorations to the ex-chancellor's.

'Lovely! Now if you'd all like to follow me,' Marie said, moving on.

'When is the baby due?' asked Achim with an eye on her belly.

'A fortnight.'

'Has the dad made a cradle yet?'

Marie didn't answer.

'Is he not much of a handyman?' said Achim. He was a gifted quantum chemist, but not so gifted when it came to reading human emotions.

'He decided not to play a part in our lives,' said Marie bitterly.

'Oh, please forgive me,' said Achim. 'I'll just take my foot out of my mouth.' He attempted to mime this action, but could only lift his leg halfway up. To Putin it looked as if his master was about to leave his mark right there and then. The pug went scurrying for cover.

To change the subject, Marie pointed to the small church. 'Balduin von Baugenwitz left his trace in St Petri Church too,' she said.

'Let me guess,' said Achim. 'He impaled nuns, priests and monks in there?'

'Not quite. But he did crucify them. What's more, over one hundred years later, Pastor Egidius Gleim spent his life looking into Adelheid von Baugenwitz's death. He came to the conclusion that she hadn't killed herself but was pushed by someone else.'

'Was Egidius an intelligent man?' Angela found herself wondering whether the pastor was another Sherlock Holmes type.

'Yes, but he was slightly odd too.'

'In what way?'

'They say he used to like ringing the church bell when he was drunk. Stark naked.'

'You call that *slightly* odd?'

'By the standards of pastors, yes.'

'In that case,' asked Angela, 'who pushed the woman from the tower, according to Egidius?'

'Balduin von Baugenwitz's first wife.'

Angela couldn't help imagining Katharina von Baugenwitz likewise pushing her replacement from the church tower. She banished the thought. As Sherlockella she was developing an over-fertile imagination. Deploying the authoritative tone she had perfected when dismissing British claims that all the benefits of Europe could be retained while leaving the EU, she said, 'Shall we go up to the castle now? I'd like to find out more about it – and to offer my condolences to the family.' Angela hoped that Marie, steeped as she was in the history of the place, might know about a secret passage in the wine cellar.

'I… I don't want to go there,' said the guide.

'Why not?'

'I grew up there.' Seeing Angela's confusion, she added, 'In East German times the castle was a children's home.'

So the poor woman was an orphan!

'I was a foundling.'

Angela looked at her sympathetically.

'It might sound bad. But I had a good time there. The director of the home, Thea, was an angel.' Marie gave a sad smile, like somebody thinking of a beloved person they've lost.

'What happened to her?'

'After reunification the von Baugenwitz family demanded the castle back. In 1994 we children were assigned to different homes in Brandenburg. I was six years old at the time. And Thea lost her job. She never recovered... Seven years later she took her own life. On the railway line to Berlin.'

'And that's why you don't want to go to the castle anymore,' said Angela.

'I hate the von Baugenwitz family!' said Marie with sudden venom.

This seemed to make it unlikely that Philipp was the child's father, thought Angela. Yet Marie could have another motive for killing the baron: revenge for the death of her beloved foster mother. And even though Angela told herself it was indecent to suspect a friendly, likeable woman who was clearly having a hard time of it, a small part of her whispered, 'Treat murder cases like boards of bank directors: start by assuming everyone's guilty.'

17

During the rest of the tour they learned several more interesting things about the history of Klein-Freudenstadt. Mostly these concerned Pastor Egidius Glen, who had not only rung the church bells in his birthday suit, but also marched naked at the head of the 1769 hunger revolt against the aristocracy. This eccentric fellow had almost succeeded in gaining farmers the rights to their rulers' estates throughout the whole Uckermark region. But the baron at the time, Walter von Baugenwitz – he who would die twenty years later in the musket duel – deployed mercenaries in a cloak-and-dagger operation which ended with Egidius being thrown into the lake, weighed down with holy relics from his church.

'Do you seriously think that nice woman is a suspect?' said Achim as they made their way towards the castle.

'Every murderer is someone's old friend. One must not mix up sentiment and reason,' said Angela a little pompously, quoting her favourite Belgian detective.

'But, Muffinella, this isn't politics. Or an Agatha Christie book. Not everyone has two faces!'

Angela felt slightly ashamed.

'As far as I'm concerned,' Achim went on, 'it can only have been Alexa von Baugenwitz. She's always wanted to sell the castle and now it belongs to her. That gives her a crystal-clear motive.'

'Yes, that is certainly plausible,' said Angela, privately reflecting that simple solutions were rare in life.

'But then again, what about Katharina von Baugenwitz? There must have been a time when she and Philipp were very much in love. After all he had a tattoo of her name.'

'And how exactly do you know that?' said Achim.

'From the post-mortem. It was on his bottom.'

'You're telling me you saw the baron's bottom?'

'Surely you aren't jealous about a dead man's bum?' said Mike.

'The point is,' said Angela, 'it is possible that Katharina never got over her husband leaving her for Alexa.'

'Well in that case,' said Achim, 'she might still try

82

to push her successor from the church tower. Maybe the murders that happened centuries ago are repeating themselves.'

'Do you think so?' said Angela, who'd already considered this scenario.

'That would certainly be inventive.'

'Perhaps we should warn Alexa von Baugenwitz?' said Achim. 'If we're taking this idea seriously, that is.'

'But if you're right and she's the murderer,' said Angela, 'we'd merely be letting her know that we're sniffing around.'

'True. A veritable dilemma,' commented Achim.

'In my opinion there's another – even more plausible – explanation,' said Mike, as they all stepped up to the castle gate.

'Fruit-seller Angela?' said Former-Leader-of-the-Free-World Angela.

'No. That it was a suicide after all. So far there has been precisely zero evidence to the contrary.'

'Well,' said Angela pressing the bell, 'we're here to find some.'

'Excuse me, but may I ask how exactly you're planning to do that?' asked the bodyguard.

By way of an answer Angela removed the gauntlet from her bag and pointed to the metal hexagram-shaped attachment. 'This could be the key to a secret passage.'

'You stole the gauntlet?!' said Achim in total astonishment. Or more precisely, he was four-fifths astonished and one-fifth outraged.

'Why are you getting so agitated?'

'Because… because it's so unlike you!'

'This is a murder investigation.'

'You've changed,' Achim told her.

Angela had to admit that this was true.

'And I'm not sure if I like it.' Achim decided he was no longer outraged but instead five-eighths confused and three-eighths disappointed.

Before Angela could reply, the electric gate opened. She placed the gauntlet back in her bag and, for the first time since the body had been discovered, found herself thinking about something other than the investigation. Was Achim saying he was worried about what would happen to their marriage if she changed? Should she be worried too?

18

Pia the teenager was sitting on the fountain steps, staring at her phone.

'Does she ever take her eyes off that thing?' said Achim.

'She's just a child of her time,' said Angela. 'They read books until puberty. After that it's nothing but screens.'

'I'm happy I was a child of another time.'

Everything's relative, thought Angela as she remembered her own childhood in East Germany. Even if all that glistered wasn't gold these days, there was both more glistering and more gold today than in the past. She felt a brief moment of pride at her own small contribution to this more glistering world. It didn't last long.

'Hello, Muffin,' said Pia, nodding towards Angela without looking up from her mobile.

'I'm Muffin,' said Achim.

'Hello, Muffin,' she repeated, still not looking up.

'She's Muffinella,' explained Achim, gesturing towards his wife. Not for the first time, Angela wondered why he always had to be so pedantic.

'Hello, Muffinella,' said the girl, finally looking up with a grin. She pointed at Mike. 'So who's that? Your over-sized Muffin baby?'

'That's Mike Franz, our bodyguard.'

'Hello, large Muffin Baby.'

Mike gave her a look that would have frozen the blood in the veins of most people, but Pia kept grinning.

'And that thing there,' Pia said, pointing at Putin who, exhausted by all the walking, was lying at Angela's feet, 'must be Muffin Baby's little brother.'

Before Mike could respond, Angela raised a hand. 'My heartfelt sympathy,' she said to Pia.

'You mean because of Philipp?'

'Yes, it must be very painful for you.' After all, she thought, the baron had been Pia's stepfather for a while – before the divorce from her mother, Katharina.

'I've suffered more,' said Pia. 'Like once when the wifi in the castle went down for like, three whole hours.'

'I'm guessing you didn't like him?'

'No shit, Sherlock.'

Achim was torn between pointing out that 'Sher-lockella' was the correct form of address and giving the teenager a good ticking off. In the event he did neither because Angela said, 'Muffin, I think Putin's thirsty.'

Achim began to fill his water bottle from the fountain. Angela was about to tell him it wasn't normal practice to let the dog drink out of the same bottle as its owner, when Pia asked, 'Is the pug called Putin?'

'Yes, he is.'

'Sick! So what do you call his ticks? Orban and Assad?'

Angela couldn't help laughing. The girl was politically astute and had a good sense of humour. 'I call them Conspiracy and Theorist,' she said.

Now it was Pia's turn to laugh. An unexpected moment of intimacy opened up between them. Angela tried to exploit this to find out more about the aristocratic family. 'Why couldn't you stand Philipp?'

'Guess.'

'Because he hurt your mother by leaving her for Alexa?'

'That too.'

'Too?'

'When she was married to him it was like I didn't exist,' said Pia. 'He didn't give a shit about me. He never accepted me as a daughter. And when he left Mum, the bastard just ghosted me.'

'How old were you then?' Angela said, full of sympathy. Pia held all ten fingers up, stuck her AirPods in her ears and stared at her phone again. Angela was left standing awkwardly beside her. She'd have liked to offer some words of comfort, but clearly Pia didn't want to hear them.

'What brings you here?' called the voice of Alexa von Baugenwitz. Angela turned around, half-expecting to see the actress with another glass of champagne in her hand.

Instead she was standing stone-cold sober in front of the castle in a widow's mourning dress: grey blouse, long black skirt and matching black jacket. Her eyes weren't swollen with tears, and she didn't even seem particularly hungover. She looked composed. Like an aristocrat at home in the castle that now belonged to her.

'If anyone killed the old goat, it was her,' whispered Mike.

Angela was inclined to agree. As sole heir, the widow was surely the chief suspect.

She approached Alexa. 'We wanted to express our condolences.'

'Go on, then.'

'We can hardly imagine what a terrible loss this must be for you. Please accept our—'

'Yes, yes, I get it,' cut in Alexa.

Angela was shocked by the woman's lack of decorum. Was this grief at work, or something more sinister?

'You can go now.'

Obviously Angela couldn't go; she was desperate to find the secret passage, open it using the gauntlet and then announce with a complacent smile, 'You see? It was a murder after all!' She thought fast. 'First, I would like to offer my sympathy to Katharina von Baugenwitz.'

'What business is it of that sad old bag?' said Alexa.

Pia, who could evidently hear everything despite her earbuds, leapt to her feet. 'How dare you!' she said.

'How dare I what?' sneered Alexa.

'The only person who's allowed to insult my mother is me! You're nothing compared to her. You aren't even a proper aristocrat!'

From these words Angela guessed that either Pia's mother had blue blood, or the father who'd died in the car accident. Or perhaps both.

Alexa was visibly seething with anger but she forced herself not to swallow the bait. 'Mark my words,' she yelled at Angela. 'That old bitch is to blame for Philipp's death!'

19

'Katharina?' said Angela. She felt a combination of alarm and excitement – was Alexa confirming that it was indeed a murder?

'Of course.'

'Did she kill him?'

Pia snorted and made a gesture that expressed her low opinion of the adults present.

'You could put it that way,' said Alexa, without deigning to glance at the girl.

'Katharina refused to get rid of the hemlock he killed himself with.' She pointed to a bed full of nothing but the small, white-flowering plants that Achim had noticed during the festival. 'She would always say, "They're part of this castle's history." History, history, history – the stupid cow thinks of nothing else!'

'Well, not everyone wants to spend every waking moment thinking about money!' said Pia.

She got up and headed for the castle gate without saying goodbye. Angela wondered where she was going. What on earth did the girl do here when she wasn't fiddling around with her mobile?

She turned back to the widow. 'Where can I find Katharina?'

'She's doing an inventory of the wine,' said Alexa with scorn. 'Even on a day like this all she thinks about is business.'

So Katharina was in the vault where the body had been found. What a stroke of luck! Angela knew that even the best detectives needed good fortune from time to time. Now it was up to her to take advantage of it to look for the secret passage.

'Why are you smiling?' asked Alexa.

Angela felt caught out. If she wanted to become a really good detective she had to remember to use her poker face – like that time when Gaddafi had been raving about his sexy female bodyguards. 'I'm sorry,' she lied. 'I was just thinking of your excellent wine.'

'Whatever. Anyway, I don't accept your condolences.'

Angela was taken aback. Her condolences hadn't exactly been heartfelt, but she thought she'd done a passable job of feigning them. Ordinary life was proving more and more challenging.

'You look down on me like all the rest of them,' continued Alexa. She was about to spit on the beautiful white pebbles, but decided against it. 'I've got to talk to the investor now,' she said more calmly, taking her mobile from her handbag. 'He's on his way from the airport.' Without saying goodbye, she walked off in the direction of the park.

'I hereby confirm my hypothesis that they lack manners around here,' said Achim.

'She's the murderer, a hundred per cent,' said Mike.

'First things first,' said Angela. 'Let's find out if it really was a murder!' She took the gauntlet from her bag with a playful flourish.

'Hey!' All three of them turned around to see Katharina von Baugenwitz striding quickly towards them from the castle. 'May I ask what you are doing with the gauntlet from Philipp's armour?'

20

When politicians are caught with their trousers down, they have a variety of techniques for dealing with the situation. German ministers might say, 'In due course I will give a statement about the gauntlet to the relevant parliamentary committee.' Russian premiers might say, 'Let's see if you're still so interested in the gauntlet when you're in prison.' And a certain former US president might say, 'Gauntlet? That's not a gauntlet! You're a gauntlet!'

In the past Angela had always wheeled out her spokesman for these occasions. He'd started out in his role an elegant, rosy-cheeked man, but now looked so grey-faced that you'd think he was straight out of a black-and-white film. Apparently he'd joined a silent order the day after her retirement.

Right now there was no spokesman, so Angela opted for candour. 'I believe this gauntlet is special,' she said.

'Special?' Katharina sounded genuinely curious.

'Look at this protrusion.'

Katharina took a closer look. 'A hexagram. That

would be typical of Balduin – the torturer. But what does it mean?'

'I believe it is the key to a secret passage.'

'What sort of secret passage?'

'Maybe one that leads to the wine cellar. I mean, it was originally used as a dungeon, wasn't it? And perhaps Balduin used it to go in and out of the castle unnoticed.'

'You really are incredible!' said Katharina.

As a politician Angela had learned the hard way that people only paid you compliments when they wanted to butter you up. The first time she'd met Helmut Kohl, for example, he'd made a flattering remark about her hairstyle – and in less than a minute she'd signed up to his deal on nuclear waste disposal. But Angela was no longer a politician. She was an amateur sleuth, and she found herself lapping up Katharina's esteem for her powers of deduction. 'Incredible in what way, exactly?' she asked with a smile.

She was expecting something like: 'Balduin's descendants have lived here for centuries without ever discovering a secret passage. Yet you found it immediately. You must have an extraordinary mind!'

Instead she heard: 'Balduin's descendants have lived here for centuries without ever discovering a secret passage. And you seriously believe you have done so now? What arrogance!'

'Well, er...' Angela felt ashamed.

'Not just that – you come here with this nonsense on a day of mourning!'

Now Angela felt almost as bad as when she'd realised that Helmut Kohl hadn't meant it about her hair.

91

'And without even offering your condolences!'

'I did! To your daughter and Alexa. And of course I'd like to offer my sincere—'

'Please... stop!' Katharina burst into tears. 'My Philipp is dead!'

Her Philipp?

Did she still harbour feelings for him?

At any rate she was the only one who was shedding tears over his death. Pia and Alexa hadn't exactly seemed grief-stricken.

'It's alright, it's alright...' said Katharina, composing herself. She was on the point of wiping her nose on her sleeve, but then seemed to recall that this would be unbecoming of an aristocrat such as herself. Angela would have liked to offer her a tissue but all she had was a poo bag, which she knew lacked the correct physical properties. She glanced at Achim, who read her thoughts but merely shrugged. It was Mike who whipped out a monogrammed handkerchief. Angela recognised it as the cloth he used to clean his pistol. He handed it to Katharina, who blew her nose loudly and profusely before handing it back to the bodyguard, who tried to conceal his reluctance to handle it without protective gear.

Angela wondered whether now was the moment to ask permission to snoop around in the dungeon for a secret door. She had just decided against it when Alexa von Baugenwitz returned. 'The investor will be here soon,' she told Katharina.

'Well it's about time you hopped into bed with him. Philipp has been dead for almost a whole day now.'

'Sticks and stones may break my bones, but words—' said Alexa.

'You're delighted Philipp's dead. Now you can flog everything off!'

'… can never hurt me,' continued Alexa unconvincingly.

'You hated Philipp!'

'Is that surprising? The way he cheated on me…!'

Angela couldn't help but think of the pregnant Marie. Much as she'd like to, she couldn't quite dismiss the possibility that she had been one of the baron's lovers.

'At least you know what it feels like now,' said Katharina bitterly.

'But I never said I wished he was dead. Like you did when he left you for me!'

'Ladies, ladies…!' Achim hated conflict, which was one reason why he preferred dealing with quanta than people. Their behaviour was just as unpredictable, but they were nowhere near as bad-tempered.

The two women both shot him a 'stay out of this' look. But Achim, who was far better at reading quantum diagrams than people's faces, persevered. 'Ladies!' he said again. 'How about we all calm down?'

Before Achim could make things even worse, Angela intervened: 'I think we'd better go.'

There would be another opportunity to look for the secret passage, she thought. Perhaps it was better for the time being to withdraw in order to ponder all the information and clues.

Just as the small troop were leaving, Katharina barked, 'The gauntlet stays here!'

Angela turned back. What should she do? The item was crucial for her investigation! She felt like saying, 'Gauntlet? What gauntlet? You're a gauntlet!'

'She thinks it's the key to a secret door,' Katharina told her successor.

'Secret door?' said Alexa. 'There's something wrong with that woman!'

'That's what I said.'

The pair of them gave Angela a nasty smile. It wasn't at all nice when they were on the same side.

'Hand it over then,' said Alexa.

Defeated, the ex-chancellor relinquished the gauntlet. 'And now – goodbye!'

Angela, Achim, Mike and Putin headed off back down the hill. With every step Angela became angrier and angrier at the thought that she was departing the castle without anything tangible. Real detectives never left without a new lead. Take Inspector Columbo, for example. He would always catch witnesses and suspects off guard, just as they were relaxing because they thought they were rid of him. She must be able to do the same – confront them with some unexpected question. Yes! Angela knew exactly what to ask!

She turned to see Katharina and Alexa making for different entrances to the castle. Evidently neither wanted to spend another second in each other's presence. 'Excuse me!' she called out. 'Just one more thing…'

Angela trotted back up to the two women, followed by Achim and Mike, who were wondering what was coming next. 'Who is "a"?' she asked.

The women looked blank.

Angela went over to one of the small ornamental trees, broke off a branch and drew the 'ɑ' as best she could in the gravel. 'This was the last thing the baron wrote on a piece of paper in the dungeon just before he died.'

Both women turned white.

Angela fixed them with her most piercing stare. Miss Marple would have been proud of her.

'Do you know what it means?' she asked.

'No,' the two women stammered almost in unison.

'Then I shan't detain you any longer.' Angela turned her back and walked away in high satisfaction. From their reaction it was clear that both Alexa and Katharina knew exactly what the 'ɑ' stood for. And that, she concluded, in all likelihood meant that one of the two was the killer, while the other had just realised she was standing next to a murderer.

21

Back home, Angela and Mike sat at the rustic dining table tucking into the ex-Chancellor's freshly baked butter cake. Achim was on all fours, trying to teach Putin a new trick.

'Paw! Paw! Paw!' he said.

'Muffin, how many more times are you going to say "Paw?", asked Angela.

'Until he gives me his paw. *Paw!*'

Achim demonstrated what he wanted the pug to do. Putin looked perplexed. His expression said: 'My master's a few dog biscuits short of a treat.'

95

Angela nudged the cake towards Mike. 'Go on, have another piece,' she said temptingly.

Mike agonised. Deep within his soul the voice of reason fought uselessly with appetite's siren song. 'It would be my fourth!'

Angela rolled her eyes and shovelled another large piece of butter cake onto the bodyguard's plate. He didn't protest, but for the moment his fork stayed where it was.

'Cream?' Angela knew that Mike liked whipped cream even more than cake. Without waiting for an answer she deposited a generous spoonful on top of the cake. The sight of it crushed the last vestiges of Mike's resistance.

'Oh well, just for today I'll eat, drink and be merry!'

Angela was delighted. She was justly proud of her butter cake, even if she would have actually preferred to make a fruit cake. Out of principle, though, she had boycotted her namesake's stall, and the fruit from the small village shop was of far lower quality. Also, most of its produce came from halfway around the world. So if Angela were to bake another fruit cake, not only would it taste worse, she'd feel guilty about its carbon footprint. Not for the first time she wished she could pin the murder on the fruit-seller, but Alexa and Katharina were clearly the chief suspects. And of the two Alexa had both the strongest motive – as the sole heir – and the flimsiest alibi. She could easily have faked her booze-induced coma on the chaise longue. Yes – surely the 'a' must stand for her name.

But then... what about Katharina? She gave the impression she'd never got over having been abandoned by Philipp. And his desire to sell the castle was clearly anathema to her. But why would she want her successor, Alexa, to inherit? It didn't make sense. Unless she'd poured hemlock into the chalice in the heat of the moment, without thinking of the consequences? The very hemlock she herself had insisted still grow in the castle grounds…

Angela considered the ex-wife's alibi. Just before the murder Katharina and Lena had carried out an inspection for insurance purposes. Had the policewoman been at Katharina's side the whole time? Should she question her?

No. There was someone else who should do that.

'Mike?'

'Please! No more cake!'

Setting the last wedge on his plate, Angela said, 'What are you up to this evening?'

'First I'm going to disinfect my pistol-cleaning cloth. After that I'll clean my pistol. Then I'll watch my favourite series, *24*.' He raised a forkful of butter cake to his mouth. 'Finally, I'll begin my 24-day fast.'

'Oh, that's a shame. Lena asked me to tell you that she'd love to meet you in the gin bar tonight.'

As it happened, Angela wasn't one hundred per cent sure that the policewoman was still on for the date. Her behaviour later on in the evening had been really quite strange. Almost as if she knew something about the murder… Could she even be caught up in it herself?

It appeared Philipp had shot her by mistake while out hunting – was that enough to turn her into a killer? It was certainly possible, especially if the injury was more than a 'graze', as he'd called it. Or she might have had something going with the baron. After all, it wasn't yet clear who Philipp had cheated on Alexa with.

At the very least Lena would be able to say if she'd been with Katharina at the time the killing took place. And if she had been, that would also be an alibi for her.

'Did Lena really say that?' asked Mike.

'She did.'

'But… I'm busy!'

'You just told me you were going to watch television.'

'Oh, er, hmm… it's sort of training…'

'Training?'

'Well, the Jack Bauer character in the series is an agent and one can learn a lot from him, like—' Mike stopped short, seeing the broad smile on Angela's face.

'It'll do you good to talk to someone new,' said Angela. She hoped Lena didn't have anything to do with the murder. Mike was set to be her bodyguard in Klein-Freudenstadt for a long time yet; he needed to make friends. Something that, despite her own efforts, Angela had singularly failed to do.

'Why are you looking so sad all of a sudden?' said Mike.

Angela was taken aback. She'd spent decades training herself not to let her emotions show. The only person who'd ever been able to read her feelings was Achim, even though he freely admitted that everything he knew about interpreting facial expressions came from studying Spock on 'Star Trek'. Now, after just six weeks in Klein-Freudenstadt, Mike was able at a glance to penetrate her façade. And that wasn't the only way she'd changed. For years she hadn't once thought about her ability to forge close friendships, yet now she seemed to be worrying about it constantly.

She shook herself in an attempt to banish the thought. 'I'm fine,' she said, forcing a smile. Mike clearly didn't believe her – Klein-Freudenstadt had well and truly ruined her famous poker face – but he didn't probe further. He had other problems.

'Lena must be fifteen years younger than me,' he said.

'It's all about how old you feel inside,' said Angela.

'But… I'm not very good at talking to women.'

He wasn't lying. In any case, Angela had no idea what people chatted about on a first date these days. Probably not nuclear magnetic resonance, like her and Achim. Since nothing better came to mind, she said, 'You could talk about your hobbies.'

'Lifting weights? Or… I do like knitting sleeves for my guns. That could be good.'

'No, it wouldn't be good. What about paying her compliments instead?'

'Yes! I could tell her she has a wonderfully broad back!'

'Not exactly what I had in mind.'

'Her squint is cute?'

'Anything else?'

'Her blue eyes make me think of the Dumpfsee?'

'Better… But perhaps go for a nicer-sounding lake.'

Angela liked Mike's awkward sincerity. If Lena was looking for an honest man in her life rather than a phoney – i.e. the complete opposite of the baron, with whom she may or may not have had something going – then Mike could be just the ticket.

99

'Don't worry,' she said encouragingly. 'You'll find the right words.'

'Do you think?'

'He did with me.' Angela nodded towards Achim, who was in the garden demonstrating to Putin how to lie on his back and stick all four limbs into the air.

Mike laughed. 'In that case, maybe there is some hope!'

'And once you've broken the ice,' said Angela, 'you can ask her if she was with Katharina for the whole hour leading up to Philipp's death.'

'You mean I'm going on a date with Lena so I can interrogate her on your behalf?'

'I'm sure you can do your duty without neglecting romance,' said Angela, a little doubtfully.

'You're the strangest boss I've ever had,' said Mike, with a shake of the head.

'You're not the first person to have said that.'

'Well, I'd better get myself ready!' Mike rose to his feet. 'I hope I find a pair of trousers that still fits.'

He left the room, happier and more excited than Angela had ever seen him. But suddenly she felt a twist of anxiety. What if Lena ended up breaking his heart? What if she was involved in the murder after all?

22

The evening sun set across the market square. If Mike hadn't felt so tense he could have enjoyed the view. Beneath the tough-guy exterior, he was a romantic. He adored sunsets, love songs and nature. When he'd watched the film *Titanic* with his ex-wife, Mike had sobbed more than her. Then again, that wasn't hard: Nicole made White Walkers from *Game of Thrones* look like cry-babies. Soon after the birth of their daughter Lilly, she'd filed for divorce and was granted custody of the child. Mike's irregular work hours and long trips abroad were what swayed the judge. Now that he finally had a quieter job he hoped he'd be able to gradually rebuild his relationship with his daughter.

Mike stopped a few steps away from Aladdin's Gin. Was everything as it should be? Suit, tie, socks. He'd put on his best clothes, though these were barely distinguishable from the rest of his attire, since Mike's wardrobe housed seven copies of the same outfit, one for every day of the week. And one pair of Mickey Mouse underpants, which his daughter had given him as a birthday present five years ago.

He nervously adjusted the sleeves of his shirt beneath the arms of his jacket. He felt a strong urge to turn around and go home. Since the failure of his marriage he no longer trusted his taste in women. Better to stay single with Netflix than to be hurt again. But he was on a mission for his boss this evening, so chickening out was not an option. If he returned to the small timber-frame house empty-handed, she'd be sure to find a way to punish him. She might even cut his cake allowance!

With these thoughts running through his mind, Mike entered Aladdin's Gin. The bar looked roughly how German bar-owners imagine a gin bar in New York to be: leather benches, wooden bar and shelves of bottles with

English labels. And it was full: couples, groups of friends, more than a few teenagers who looked well under eighteen... It seemed they weren't too fussed about the drinking laws round here. And there, sitting at a small table in the corner, was Lena.

In an elegant red dress, with a green leather jacket around her shoulders, she looked stunning. When she caught his eye, Mike felt himself freeze to the spot, but she gave him such a friendly wave that he somehow managed to make his way to her table.

'I'm so pleased you came,' she said.

'Hmm.' He couldn't manage any more: her freckled face, that wonderful red hair...

'Shall we order something? They do a great gin basil smash here. Or maybe you'd prefer the cucumber smash?'

'Uh...' The colour of her eyes...!

Lena pretended to examine the drinks menu. 'Unfortunately I don't think they have "uh",' she said.

Mike knew he had to think of something, but what? What had the boss said? He should pay her compliments.

'You've got a cute little squint,' he said.

'What?' Lena looked as if she couldn't decide whether to feel flattered or offended.

'Your eyes are like the Dumpfsee,' said Mike. 'And your shoulders are impressively broad.'

'Compliments aren't your strong point, are they?'

'Sorry.' Mike felt embarrassed to his core.

'No need to apologise – I appreciate the effort!' she said. 'You're sweet.'

'That's better,' said Lena. 'I'll get us a gin.' Mike watched in fascination as she wandered over to the bar. She was so much nicer than his ex-wife Nicole. Admittedly, so were the contestants in a Mexican dogfight, but still.

When Lena leaned over the bar Mike saw her grimace in pain. Then she held the shoulder that was covered by the leather jacket. Had she injured herself? The baron had mentioned 'grazing' her with a shot. He could ask Lena about this – it might even start a proper conversation! But first he had to investigate Katharina's alibi.

Lena was smiling as she came back to the table, carrying two basil smashes. Mike tried to return the smile.

'We'll have to work on that smile,' Lena said, so sweetly that Mike's face actually relaxed. 'See, better already.'

The two of them clinked glasses. The gin trickled down Mike's throat and he began to feel at ease.

'Yesterday evening—' he began.

'Yes?' Lena's expression seemed to cloud over.

'You were with Katharina von Baugenwitz to do the inspection for the insurance, weren't you?'

'Is this your idea of romantic conversation?'

Lena's enchanting smile had vanished. Mike realised he had to get this alibi thing over and done with quickly before the evening was ruined.

'So she couldn't have been with the baron when he died?'

'No, she couldn't have.'

So Lena was Katharina von Baugenwitz's alibi. As far as Mike was concerned this was sufficient information for his boss. The evening could move on.

'Why do you want to know?' asked Lena. 'Why are you even interested in that bastard's death?'

Mike was taken aback. 'Bastard?'

'He shot me.'

'I thought the bullet just grazed you.'

'That's what he likes to tell people. In truth he riddled my shoulder blade with shot. And put an end to my sporting career.'

'Oh no! What was your sport?'

'Archery. I was quite good, actually. I qualified for the Olympics.'

'The Olympics! Wow!'

'But it all came to nothing,' said Lena. 'I couldn't go to the games because of the injury.' She took a sip of her drink and now her voice was steeped in bitterness. 'To get back to my former level I need a special operation. With Dr Hickman in Fort Lauderdale. He looks after Serena Williams.'

'When are you having the operation?'

'Three years too late.'

'I don't understand.'

'It costs 25,000 euros. Which I've only just scraped together now.' She took a bigger sip.

'Surely the baron ought to have paid for it. As compensation,' said Mike.

'He should have, but he didn't.'

'Why not?'

'Because his lawyers were better than mine. I only got 875 euros.' Lena finished her gin in one large gulp. Mike sensed how angry she felt at the dead man. And as far as he was concerned she had every right to be angry. Three years of pain. Her sporting career in tatters...

'I'm sorry,' she said, wiping away the tears on her sleeve. 'Blubbing like this on a first date...'

'Don't worry. We can talk about everything. Even things that make you cry. Or if you prefer we can talk about something else. Anything. I really do like talking to you.'

'Whoah! When you string together a few sentences like that, it's quite impressive,' said Lena, smiling through the tears.

Mike grinned.

'I like your smile.'

Mike felt all warm inside.

'And that's why,' she continued, blowing her nose, 'we ought to—'

'Get another gin?'

'Exactly. And then, like all sensible people on their first date, we'll just talk about music and television. Emotional wounds don't crop up until date number five. Two dates after the first sex.'

Mike's expression was so comical that Lena forgot about her troubles and actually managed a laugh.

23

In vain Angela tried to concentrate on the new biography of Shakespeare she was reading. For the twelfth time her eyes took in the sentence *Some historians believe that Shakespeare was in fact a woman by the name of Emilia Bassano*, without her brain even starting to consider the implications of this theory. It wasn't just that she was thinking about the case. In the background her husband was playing his weekly game of Scrabble with his friend Tommy via Skype. Achim had used all his letters to make PHENOXY, not only scoring a triple-word bonus but adding the P to the already-existing ALLIUM to form another equally obscure word denoting an ecclesiastical vestment. He was actually squealing with delight. Meanwhile, Angela was focusing on another letter – the mysterious 'α' – and coming up with a dizzying array of possibilities. There was 'Alexa von Baugenwitz', 'Angela the fruit woman' and even 'Amadeus, Lena' (Amadeus, she had discovered, was the policewoman's surname).

'PANTIES!' yelled Achim in triumph, having just found a use for the second P that had come into his possession.

When he and Tommy were in a Scrabble frenzy it could go on for hours. Angela decided to cut her losses. She gathered up the pug and took him out for his evening walk.

No sooner was she in the street with Putin than she felt better. The last rays of the setting sun bathed the world in a golden glow, and moreover she was out without a bodyguard. For the first time in over sixteen years! It felt so liberating! If only she could dance like Julie Andrews in *Mary Poppins*, Angela thought, she would whirl nimbly across the cobbles with Putin. But neither she nor her dog were exactly nimble, so she merely wandered buoyantly down the little street to the market square, where the last shops were closing and, at the outside café tables, the inhabitants of Klein-Freudenstadt were switching from cappuccino to beer or spritzers.

'Hey, Muffinella! How's it going?'

Angela turned around. Pia von Baugenwitz was sitting at one of the tables with her smartphone. The sight of the blue-haired teenager muted Angela's good mood.

'I'm fine. How about you?'

'Banging. I've got a beer, a joint and something to celebrate.'

She didn't seem to be feeling any grief at all.

'What is there to celebrate?'

'My Insta has just hit 300,000 followers.'

Angela had never been a social media pro herself. Other people had always looked after her online presence. All the same she knew enough about it to be able to say, 'That's a pretty decent number.'

'Especially when they're the right types.'

'And your followers are the right types?'

'They're all sheltered rich kids who feel misunderstood. They buy everything I recommend.'

'You earn money by advertising?'

'Forty grand a month.'

Angela was astonished. That was far more than she'd been paid in her old job.

'My I'm-a-rebellious-aristo routine is remarkably successful. I'm a role model for all the losers.'

'Routine?'

'Do you think I dye my hair blue because I think it looks good?'

'You do it to strengthen your image as a rebel?'

'I like to call it a "brand", but yes.'

'Do you still go to school?'

'Hey, boomer – I earn 40,000 per month!'

Angela didn't know whether to be impressed or repulsed by Pia. What couldn't be denied, however, was that the girl might prove a valuable source of information. In an attempt to get closer to her, she said, 'If you like we could do a selfie together for your account.'

'Nah.'

Angela was surprised. Normally she was swamped when she made such an offer. Had her popularity plummeted since she'd become a pensioner? If so, how did she feel about it? She might like to think of herself as devoid of vanity, but was self-aware enough to know that this was not the case.

'You're too old and basic for my followers.'

'I understand.'

'And not stylish enough.'

'I understand.'

'A photo with you would probably lose me a few hundred fans.'

'I said, I understand!'

Pia beamed at her. She took far too much pleasure in provocation.

'Tell me,' Angela said, opting for a direct approach instead of trying to make friends with the girl, 'is Alexa now going to sell the castle to the highest bidder?'

'Well the Yank didn't waste much time getting here.'

'So you think she's greedy too?'

'Pure gold-digger.'

This coincided with Angela's own hunch.

'But the silly cow is ignoring the really big money,' said Pia.

'What do you mean?'

'I mean she's happy with the twenty million from the sale of the castle. And Philipp was just as dumb. Even when he was still married to Mum he always rejected her plan, which would have allowed them to restore the property.'

'What plan?'

'After the war the von Baugenwitz family had to hand over a lot more than just the castle to the communists. In every second museum in Brandenburg there's art belonging to the family that was confiscated by the GDR. If you add it all up it's worth at least 200 million.'

'And these works of art weren't given back after reunification?'

'No, because supposedly old Ferdinand von Baugenwitz collaborated with the Nazis.'

'And descendants of collaborators,' said Angela, 'have no legal claim on confiscated items.'

'Exactly.'

'You said that Ferdinand von Baugenwitz "supposedly" collaborated with the Nazis. Do you mean it isn't true?'

'No. Of course he did.'

'So there's no "supposedly" about it, is there?'

'Depends on your POV.'

'I'm not sure I follow you.'

'Point of view. Mum found a few historians prepared to testify the opposite. For the right fee, obviously.'

'So if the case went to court, the family would have a good chance of getting their art back?'

'Correct.'

'But Philipp wasn't interested,' continued Angela. 'He just wanted to be rid of the castle and get away from here with Alexa. Rather than spend years or even decades caught up in lawsuits. Twenty million in the hand is worth more than two hundred in the bush?'

'You're smarter than you look,' said Pia. 'But you need to work on your metaphors.'

Angela ignored this and thought about what she'd just heard. Katharina had two quite different reasons to be angry with her ex-husband. First he'd left her for the younger Alexa, having already cheated during their marriage. Then he'd rejected her plan to recover the family's works of art and restore the castle to its former glory. If their marriage hadn't broken down and he'd listened to Katharina, she might now be an incredibly rich woman. Angela was keener than ever to learn the results of Mike's investigation into her alibi. And the thought of alibis now reminded her that there was something she hadn't asked Pia.

'What were you doing, by the way, when Philipp died?'

'Really? You want to know if I've got an alibi? For his suicide?'

Angela tried to play down her suspicions. 'I'd just like to know if you saw him around the time of his death.'

'Well, I was doing an Insta livestream. To show my followers how lame a provincial wine festival is. That gives me a few hundred thousand witnesses.'

'That's good,' said Angela. She was eager to remove names from the list of suspects rather than add more.

'Want to see?'

'No, it's fine.'

'Here,' Pia said, ignoring her. She played the video, which had already received tens of thousands of views. Angela watched as Pia made fun of the guests – including her former stepfather, who she said came from 'centuries of inbreeding'. At the end, bent over a half-full bowl of punch, she declared, 'Paint stripper is the nectar of the gods compared to this stuff. That's why I always get bevved up on Dom Perignon. So should you! And don't forget: anarchy is possible, if you can get it organised!'

Angela wasn't interested in the girl's verbiage, but the video's timecode did indeed show that at the time of the murder Pia was live-streaming to her followers from the wine festival.

'If you're suggesting that Philipp was murdered – and I'll say straight out that the old fart deserved it – then it's her you should be asking for an alibi.' Pia pointed towards the market square, where the pregnant Marie was just coming out of the supermarket with two full bags of shopping.

'And the reason I say that is that she's carrying Philipp von Baugenwitz's bastard child.'

'One more derogatory word like that—' said Angela, giving the girl the threatening look she'd cultivated especially for Silvio Berlusconi.

'And what?'

'Then I'll out you as a fake to all my followers,' bluffed Angela. It was an empty threat, since all her accounts had been suspended on the day she handed over to Olaf Scholz.

Pia stared at Angela and tried to work out whether this was a bluff or not. In the end the risk to her business model must have seemed too great: 'Enjoy your evening, then. And say hi to Muffin from me.'

Angela scowled, but Pia's eyes were once more fixed on her mobile. Marie hadn't yet noticed Angela. Should she go up and ask about her alibi? That would feel low. No, she was going to leave her in peace. Putin, however, took a different view, running straight at Marie, or more accurately her shopping bags, in which he seemed to have detected something of interest. Sausage or cheese. Or chunks of herring in dill, which for some unfathomable reason he adored. Following her pug, Angela apologised to Marie: 'The little one likes his food.'

'That makes two of us,' Marie replied, putting the bags on the floor to take out a slice of ham. 'My big, fat belly isn't just because I'm pregnant.'

Angela was in two minds as to whether she should now ask the woman about the baby's father. A real detective would, no matter how shabby it made her feel. Sleuths had to be cool, analytical types, like Sherlock Holmes or Hercule Poirot. Angela could not bring herself to behave like that. All the same she didn't want to waste the opportunity to make at least some progress in her investigation.

'Did you use to play hide-and-seek in the castle when you were a child?' she asked Marie, who was giving Putin a stroke.

112

'Not just in the castle. In the gardens, by the lake, all over the grounds.'

'Did you ever come across a secret passage?'

'Sure did!' Marie said, grinning.

Angela's heart beat faster. 'Where?'

'In the boathouse by the lake behind the castle. There's a hatch in the floor. It always used to be covered by a horrid green rug.'

'Where did it lead?' Angela was barely able to contain her excitement.

'Somewhere in the castle.'

'Somewhere?'

'We only ever got to a metal door that was always locked.'

'Was there by any chance an indent in the door in the shape of a hexagram?'

'Yes!' Marie said, taken aback. 'How did you know?'

'There's one on the gauntlet from the baron's armour,' Angela said proudly. She expected Marie to look happy at Angela's having solved a puzzle from her childhood. But instead she suddenly looked uncomfortable. 'Erm… well… that's er… quite something.'

If Marie hadn't been so friendly, Angela might now have added her to the list of suspects, even though there was no connection between her name and the letter 'a'. But what had Achim said? 'We're not in politics here. Not everyone's two-faced!'

'Ow!' groaned Marie.

'What's wrong?'

'The baby's really kicking.'

'Shall I help you carry the bags home?' Angela asked. She felt maternal feelings welling up inside her. Or were they grand-maternal? At any rate they were unusual. And somehow nice. If she couldn't find a friend in Klein-Freudenstadt, then maybe someone she could help along in life a little? Angela was surprised at herself. The ideas that came into your head when you didn't spend your every waking hour engaged in politics!

'That's very kind of you, but it's not necessary,' said Marie. 'But if I ever do need help, I promise I'll ask for it.'

Angela wondered who was going to be with Marie when the child was born. The father was dead if he was Philipp von Baugenwitz, and absent if he wasn't. Marie herself was an orphan and her substitute mother, the director of the home, had died long ago. Did she have anybody to help her?

'Is someone going to be with you when you give birth?' asked Angela.

'My two best friends have left to work in the west,' said Marie sadly. 'I lived in Wiesbaden for a couple of years too. With my degree in tourism management I got a job in a travel company. But I wasn't happy there. The Uckermark is my home.'

'Oh dear, a mother shouldn't be on her own when giving birth,' said Angela. She'd only meant to express her sympathy, but Marie misconstrued her.

'Would you really?' she asked in amazement.

'Erm, who, you mean me...?' Angela stammered. It was rare for her to be lost for words, the last time being six weeks ago when Achim had said, 'Look, here's a dog

114

for you.' At the time she'd wondered what on earth she was going to do with a pug, but now she couldn't imagine being without her "mouse".'

'I'm sorry,' Marie said, 'I must have misunderstood.'

Angela could easily have let it go there. But she didn't.

Instead she heard herself say, 'If you like, I'll happily assist you at the birth.' She could scarcely believe her own words. Or that they sounded so good.

'Really?' Marie burst out laughing from relief and happiness. 'That would be fantastic. The idea of being alone with the midwife scares me to death. Frau Bunsen is so severe! And almost two metres tall. And she's got a voice like Chewbacca.'

'Chew... who?' Angela asked.

'The Wookiee.'

'The what?'

'Han Solo's friend.'

Angela's face was blank.

'From *Star Wars*.'

'Oh, I haven't seen it.'

'Then there's a real gap in your cultural knowledge.'

Angela kept her doubts to herself.

'You know what? Why don't you come over to my place tomorrow evening? We can watch it, eat crisps and drink coke.'

'Oh...' Angela was flabbergasted. She hadn't had an invitation like this in a long time. Never, in fact.

'I mean, only if you want to, of course.'

'I'd love to.'

'Great!'

The two women smiled at each other. Angela was delighted. Perhaps she would find a close friend in Klein-Freudenstadt after all. And soon there would be a little baby too, who she could shower with all manner of gifts. And bake cakes for its birthdays in the years to come. With tons of chocolate. And Smarties. Cakes that would send diabetics to their grave.

'Then the three of us will have a cosy evening together tomorrow,' said Marie, picking up her bags and starting to head off.

'Three?' said Angela, confused.

'With the baby of course!'

'Of course!'

'Adrian loves action films. They make him kick extra hard!' called Marie before disappearing into a little side street.

The joy drained from Angela like the helium from a balloon that finds the needle in a haystack. *Adrian...*

α

24

How rapidly exhilaration can fade, giving way to a troubled mind. Emotionless types like Hercule Poirot and Sherlock Holmes definitely had it easier during their investigations. Angela was so caught up in her own thoughts that she paid no attention to Putin, who was even more downcast than she was now that he'd realised he wasn't going to get a tasty chunk of herring. It was only when she heard a thundering 'What are you doing here?' that Angela was torn from her deliberations. Mike was storming towards her from Aladdin's Gin, shouting, 'I have to be with you at all times when you're outside the house!'

'But I'm not alone,' said Angela. She pointed at Putin, who was gazing trustingly at the bodyguard.

'So this is all just a big joke to you, is it?'

Seeing that she had dented his professional honour, Angela tried to de-escalate the situation. 'Nothing has happened to me.'

'But something could have!'

She began to sense this was about more than Mike's honour; it was about her as a person too. Her previous bodyguards had treated her like a Fabergé egg that mustn't break because that would be bad for their own career. Mike wasn't interested in his career. Her safety was important to him for the right reasons. It was touching.

'Promise me you'll never do this again!'

'I'm really sorry,' said Angela, hoping Mike would leave it there.

'I want you to promise!'

'Alright, if it makes you feel better, I promise.'

Mike said nothing and continued to look grim.

'What's wrong?' asked Angela.

'I don't feel better.'

'There's no more I can do.'

'Swear it.'

'What?'

'I want you to swear it.'

117

'Are you being serious?'

'Absolutely.'

'This is over the top.'

'Maybe, but I don't think so.'

Angela wasn't going to let Mike prescribe what she had to swear and what not. And certainly not in public. She'd really enjoyed being out without an escort. He ought to calm down. She thought of how some politicians were pretty casual when it came to keeping their promises. But she was different, at least when it came to genuine oaths. On the other hand she'd been pretty relaxed about bogus ones sworn to her parents when she was a girl. So, for the first time in fifty years, she crossed her fingers behind her back where only Putin could see them, and said, 'Okay, then, I swear.'

Mike gave a sigh of relief. Angela felt lighter too. But only for an instant, until she remembered Marie's words. Her baby was going to be called Adrian. And that meant it was a possibility that the baron had written down the name of his illegitimate child as a clue.

Angela was determined to rule Marie out. She concentrated on the other suspects. 'So, does Katharina have an alibi?' she asked.

'Lena was with her the whole time.'

'I see. Did you find out anything else?'

'That normal people have sex on the third date,' said Mike.

Angela looked at him in astonishment.

'Uh… Sorry. Forgive me.'

Angela smiled. Even though Mike's discoveries didn't

help Marie, Angela was pleased with him. Katharina could now be crossed off the list, as could Lena, who automatically had an alibi too. Unless the two of them were in cahoots…

No, surely that was most unlikely. Which only left Marie and Alexa.

It simply had to be Alexa!

And to establish precisely how she'd committed the murder, Angela needed to prove that you could get from the secret passage Marie had talked about into the wine cellar. And to work that out, naturally she had to try for herself. Preferably tonight!

'Why are you smiling like that?' said Mike.

'It's got nothing to do with you.'

'Promise?'

'I swear.'

Only Putin saw Angela cross her fingers again behind her back.

25

'What the devil are we doing here?' panted Achim.

'You don't believe in the devil,' panted Angela.

'What the Trump are we doing here?'

'We're crossing the dried-up castle moat in the dark.'

'I know that!' Achim didn't always love his wife's laconic humour.

Angela scrambled back up the side of the moat. She was really enjoying this cloak-and-dagger operation, albeit without actual cloak or dagger.

'If Mike finds out about this he'll go crazy.'

'Don't worry, he's fast asleep in the summer house. Besides, I'm his boss.'

'He's still going to go mad.'

'Only if he finds out, which he's not going to. What do they say? What you don't know can't make you go mad.'

'There are plenty of ignorant madmen in the world,' said Achim.

'And mad*women*.' Angela often had to correct her husband's androcentric language.

'Yes, alright. But tell me again, what are we doing? Why don't we go and look at the boathouse in the daytime?'

'Because Alexa von Baugenwitz won't let us.' Angela had now climbed up the other side of the trench. She held out her hand and helped Achim up.

'What we're doing is trespassing.'

'What we're doing is getting proof of how Alexa slipped out of the wine cellar unnoticed after she'd put hemlock into her husband's chalice. And to do that we need to go in there,' she said, pointing at the boathouse, which stood about thirty metres away.

'Are you absolutely sure it was her?'

'Yes I am.' Angela bustled resolutely onwards to her destination.

Behind her, Achim wouldn't let up. 'That means I can be about 81.4 per cent convinced.'

'What can I do to get that up to 100 per cent?'

'Talk to me more like a real Sherlockella, instead of just someone who's enjoying breaking all the rules.'

Angela felt caught out. She was indeed enjoying

breaking the rules; it took her back to her teenage years in the Free German Youth when she and a few others had secretly gone skinny-dipping at three in the morning.

'Alright, Muffin, if you like we'll go through all the suspects systematically one last time. Katharina isn't inheriting anything. Which means she doesn't benefit from Philipp's death.'

'But he cheated on her.'

'Yes but he cheated on Alexa too.'

'So what? That's beside the point. Katharina could still have murdered him out of jealousy.'

'Why not immediately then, when he began his affair with Alexa, rather than waiting several years?'

'Hmm, that isn't beside the point,' Achim had to concede.

'Let's run through the other possibilities. Pia—'

'Don't tell me you think the daughter's a suspect?'

'Not any more. At the time of the murder she had a huge amount of followers watching her Instagram livestream.'

'I'm not completely sure what that means.'

'It means she has an alibi.'

Angela peered through the window of the boathouse. She'd expected to see rowing boats, but there were only three pedalos that looked like swans. Apart from that there was some junk lying around and, as Marie had described, a horrid green rug. The hatch must be hidden beneath it!

'How about the fruit woman?' asked Achim. 'She's definitely a *bad apple*?'

'Achim,' said Angela sternly.

'Sorry.'

'It's true that the sale of the castle would mean her losing the farmland and her livelihood. But that's going to happen anyway now he's dead.'

'Maybe she didn't think of that.'

'The whole village knew Alexa wanted to flog the castle.'

Achim followed Angela into the musty boathouse. 'What if she had something going with the baron as well? I mean, he seemed to be juggling so many women – why not her too?'

'So far we only know for sure about Alexa and Katharina.'

'But there are also pointers towards Marie. He might have got her pregnant,' said Achim while Angela cast an eye around the boathouse.

'We don't know that,' said Angela.

'Have you asked her about her alibi?'

'No.'

'What makes you so sure she's innocent?'

'You said yourself that I shouldn't suspect her!'

'I'm also saying we shouldn't be snooping around here, but you're not listening to me.'

'As far as Marie is concerned, let's just call it women's intuition.'

'Women's intuition?'

'Yes. Why shouldn't I have women's intuition?'

'I've never said you didn't.'

'But?'

'Since when have you come to a firm conclusion without concrete facts?'

'Good question.'

'And since when has a true Sherlockella relied solely on her intuition?'

'There has never been a true Sherlockella before – I'm the first,' said Angela, trying to change the subject.

'You know what I mean.'

Angela did know. And she felt her detective's honour wounded.

'You need to approach this murder case analytically.'

Angela looked at her husband. He was the only person in the world she would take criticism from. Not gladly. But she took it. 'Okay, Marie goes back on the list of suspects.'

'That's better.'

From now on it wouldn't just be about catching the killer, but proving Marie's innocence!

26

'One more thing,' said Achim.

'I can hardly wait to hear it.'

'If you really want to solve this case, fall back on your true qualities.'

'My beauty?' said Angela playfully.

'I didn't mean that.'

'What, then?'

'Your razor-sharp mind. A case like this needs the old Angela, not a teenager on a Free German Youth summer camp.'

Achim knew her so well.

'But I'm having so much fun.'

'Yes,' Achim said, 'I can see that.'

Angela grabbed the torch from him and aimed the beam at the green rug. 'There's no dust on it!' she said. 'Which means the rug was moved sometime recently. Which suggests that the secret passage is still being used!'

'By the killer!'

'Please lift up the rug, Muffin.'

'Your wish is my command.' Achim whipped away the rug in one go, ruining the desired chivalric effect by almost falling over. Angela didn't notice. 'A hatch!' she exclaimed.

The very hatch that Marie had talked about. Wooden and with two handles in the middle. Grabbing one each, the couple pulled open both sides of the hatch and peered into a dark hole. Only when Angela shone the torch could they make out some extremely rusty metal rungs leading down.

'It's a good thing we're vaccinated against tetanus,' said Achim.

'That won't help if the rungs give out and we—' Angela shone the torch down as far as she could. The drop was at least five metres.

'Do you really believe this passage was used by the killer?'

'Yes.'

'Well if the rungs carried their weight then we'll be fine,' said Achim, at once embarking on his descent. Angela felt suddenly worried. If Achim injured himself in this foray she'd never forgive herself.

'Are you coming?' he called.

Angela realised something she wished she'd thought about earlier. 'I can't climb down and hold the torch at the same time,' she said.

'You don't need the torch.'

'How come?'

'There's an electric light here.'

Achim pressed a switch and at once was standing in the kind of neon glow you find in underground garages.

Leaving the torch on the rug, Angela came down the rungs. Cautiously. Very, very cautiously.

'If you fall, I'll catch you,' promised her husband.

'If I fall you'll be squashed!'

'Nonsense! You're as light as a feather.'

'Don't tell fibs.'

'You are as far as I'm concerned.'

'You old charmer,' Angela said as she reached the final rung.

'Old?'

'Okay, let's say young-at-heart charmer then.'

'That's better.'

The two of them started to make their way along the corridor. They were able to walk upright, but only because neither was particularly tall.

'Marie didn't mention lights,' said Angela. 'Maybe they were installed later.'

'So the baron could sneak away from whichever wife to visit his floozies without doing himself a mischief.'

'Nobody apart from you still uses the terms "floozies" and "doing oneself a mischief".'

'Not true.'

'Well I bet nobody else puts the two together in the same sentence.'

'You might be right there.'

'The passage,' said Angela, perplexed, 'slopes slightly upwards.'

'How far are we from the castle?'

'About fifty metres, I'd say. But if it doesn't start going downhill soon we're not going to end up in the wine cellar.'

The passage didn't start going downhill after fifty metres, nor after a hundred or two hundred. If anything, it was getting faintly steeper.

'Where are we going to come out?' asked Achim.

'No idea, but definitely not in the wine cellar,' said Angela. She could tear up her theory of the killer escaping through the secret passage.

How could she have been so wrong?

By treating a murder like one big game.

Achim was right: she had to get far more serious about all of this.

27

The passage ended at a metal door. Instead of a lock it had an indent in the form of a small hexagram.

'This confirms your theory about the gauntlet,' said Achim.

'If only I had it with me right now,' said Angela.

'That would not be good.'

'It wouldn't?'

'No, because then you'd have had to put on a metal glove last worn by a dead man.'

'I wouldn't.'

'You wouldn't?'

'No, because as a proper gentleman you'd put the gauntlet on.'

'I wouldn't.'

'You wouldn't?'

'No, because it would violate your principles of gender equality.'

'That's true,' said Angela. She turned to the problem at hand. Should they simply leave empty-handed? Or go back outside, find another place to break into the castle, steal the gauntlet and return to the metal door?

The second option sounded not only time-consuming but risky. It was one thing to sneak into a boathouse in an attempt to get into a wine cellar. A break-in was quite another. Especially as the castle had just undergone a security check. The newspaper headlines that would follow her arrest didn't bear thinking about. Stealing the gauntlet, therefore, was out of the question.

But how else where they going to get the door open? Bending down, Angela scratched the ground with her hand. It felt clayey. Even if they could mould it into a hexagram shape, it wouldn't be hard enough to work as a key. She took a closer look at the indent in the door. With her five fingertips she could reach every corner of the hexagram apart from one.

'Stick a finger into the sixth corner,' she told Achim.

'What are we trying to do?'

'Maybe if we both press hard enough it will undo the locking mechanism.'

'Okay, let's try.'

The two of them pressed, but the door didn't spring open.

'Didn't work,' said Achim.

Angela ignored him and thought again. 'The grooves of the hexagram have a counterpart on the gauntlet.'

'Which is why just pressing isn't enough,' said Achim, nodding scientifically.

'What if we fill these grooves with something else?' Angela bent down, took some clay and rubbed it into the grooves of the hexagram. When she'd finished she said, 'Let's try again.'

Once more the two of them stuck their fingers into the six corners and this time... the door clicked open.

'Gadzooks!' exclaimed Achim.

'You can say that again.'

'Gadz—'

'But you don't have to.'

Angela pushed open the door and the two of them found themselves staring at a scarlet curtain made from heavy velvet.

'No doubt,' whispered Angela, 'this material is there to hide the door from the other side.'

'Are we really doing this?' Achim suddenly felt very uneasy.

'As you said, I lack concrete facts. And that's why we have to gather more.'

'I wish I hadn't said it.'

'But you did.' Angela went to open the curtain.

'Wait!' whispered Achim, holding her arm. 'What if someone's on the other side?'

'Then that person would have already heard us.'

Angela carefully opened the curtain. They were in a baroque bedroom. To the left a huge wardrobe, on the floor antique rugs, and on the wall opposite an oil painting showing young women doing a merry round dance. In the centre of the room stood an enormous four-poster bed.

On an oak chest of drawers Angela saw a wedding photograph of Alexa and Philipp. This must have been their bedroom.

'Look,' whispered Achim, pointing at two half-full champagne flutes.

Angela went over. 'Alexa must have a lover,' she said.

'Not necessarily. The glasses could be from yesterday.'

'In that case the champagne would no longer be fizzy.'

'Then the two of them might be back any moment! We should get out of here now.'

'But we don't have all the facts yet.'

'We know that we're in somebody else's bedroom and could be caught red-handed at any second. What more facts do you need?'

'Who the lover is, for example.' Angela looked at the champagne bottle; on the label were the words ROEDERER ESTATE. 'American.'

'So?'

'Presumably that means the lover is Marc Wood, who's looking to buy the castle.'

'Fantastic. Now you know. Can we go now?'

'Just a moment.' Angela thought things through. Not only had Philipp royally cheated on Alexa, she appeared to have done the same to him. By comparison the Clintons seemed to have the perfect marriage. A day after losing her husband, Alexa was already loved up with the American investor. Were the two of them in bed together? Not just literally, but as far as the murder was concerned too?

'Can we please, *please* go?' said Achim.

'Yes,' replied Angela. For the time being she'd gathered enough facts; now she needed a bit of peace in which to set them in order. But before the two of them could take even a step back towards the curtain, they heard Alexa's voice.

'My God, Woody, that's so amazing!' she said in English.

'I'm actually going to be on the shuttle to Mars!' came the booming Texan voice of the investor in reply.

Achim and Angela looked first at the door behind which the voices could be heard, and which would open any second, then at the curtain at the other end of the room. The two scientists performed the same mental calculation and came to the same conclusion: we'll never make it!

Angela scanned the room for an elegant escape route worthy of her sleuthing idols, but without success. 'Under the bed!' she commanded.

'What?' said Achim a touch too loudly.

'Did you just hear something, Woody?' came the

anxious voice of Alexa. Just as the door opened, Angela and Achim dived beneath the bed. 'Nothing in here,' said Alexa, coming into the room.

'Maybe it was a ghost,' joked the Texan.

Angela and Achim lay on their stomachs, scarcely daring to breathe, as the lovers wandered over to the bed.

'I want you right here and now,' purred Wood.

Angela and Achim looked at each other in horror.

'Give it to me hard!' said Alexa.

Items of clothing flew rapidly to the ground as the lovers collapsed onto the bed. The mattress sank lower, and Angela, not as slim as Achim, had to squash herself into the floor to avoid her presence being detected.

Achim raised a questioning eyebrow at his wife. But she had no answer to give him. Should they stay and listen to what was about to happen? Or announce their presence, with all the consequences that would entail – of which the tabloid headlines would by no means be the worst. Angela and Achim would never be able to show their faces in Klein-Freudenstadt again. They'd have to go back to Berlin. When there was a murder to solve! And most of all, when she'd promised to assist with the birth of little Adrian!

'I'm gonna take you to Mars and back,' they heard Wood say.

Achim grimaced.

'With my big shuttle.'

Angela grimaced.

'All night long! I'm just getting my shuttle ready for liftoff.'

That settled it. 'Liftoff is cancelled!' Angela called out in English.

'Aaargh!' shrieked Alexa.

'What the fuck?' bellowed her American lover.

'The shuttle stays in the hangar!' said Angela, crawling out from beneath the bed. Achim followed suit on the other side. Alexa hid herself under the duvet in sheer terror, while the athletic, studio-tanned investor, still in his briefs, grabbed the champagne bottle in preparation for an attack. But at the last moment he stopped himself and his Texan jaw almost hit the floor: 'Angela... Merkel?'

'Yes,' said Angela, forcing a smile.

'What the... actual... fuck?'

Deftly wrapping the duvet around her body, Alexa von Baugenwitz said to her lover, 'Woody, could you please go outside?'

The American, for whom this surreal situation was clearly too much, was only too willing to oblige. He departed, still muttering, 'Angela... fucking... Merkel?'

Alexa turned to the intruders. 'What the hell are you doing here?' Her voice shook with rage.

'This question,' Achim sputtered with a bright-red face, 'is not that simple to answer, especially in a scientific sense.'

Alexa looked at him in irritation.

'If we consider the rotation of the planet, for example, we remember that Earth moves at a speed of 464 metres per second.'

'What?'

'If your bedroom weren't rotating too, we would have

simply hurtled past it. But since it is also subject to the rotation of the earth and—'

'Stop this rotation nonsense!'

Achim was indignant. 'It's not "nonsense". Without the rotation of the earth, the seas—'

'AAARGH!'

'Calm down,' said Angela.

'Calm down? Calm down? You sneaked into my bedroom. How did you get in here, anyway?'

'Through the secret passage.'

'What secret passage?'

Angela narrowed her eyes at her chief suspect. Did she really not know?

'Behind that curtain is a door,' Achim said, going over and pushing the curtain to one side to reveal the metal door.'

'What the…?' Alexa couldn't believe her eyes.

'It leads to the boathouse,' said Achim.

'And you came that way?'

'Yes.'

'Why?'

The honest answer, Angela thought, would be: 'Because we think you're a murderer and we're trying to prove that after poisoning Philipp you escaped unnoticed from the wine cellar through the secret passage. Unfortunately, however, the passage leads to your bedroom rather than to the wine cellar. Not that it makes you any less of a suspect. And the fact that the man you wish to sell the castle to is your lover provides an additional motive.'

But honesty, she deduced, would not be the best

policy here. On the other hand it was clearly no use to keep talking about the rotation of the earth. She decided on a controlled offensive. 'We believe that Philipp was murdered.'

'Murdered?' Alexa seemed shocked, though Angela couldn't help remembering that her chief suspect was an actress by trade. 'But the police say it was suicide.'

'We think that someone put the poison in his drink.'

'But the wine cellar was locked from the inside. And he was alone in there.'

'There must be a secret door.'

'But we've just established that the passage leads here.' Alexa pointed at the metal door.

'There must be another one,' said Angela, giving Alexa one of her hardest stares, which did not escape the widow's notice.

'Hold on a second… you don't seriously think that I…?'

'Well, now we know that you have a lover.'

'Philipp was always cheating on me too!'

'That also sounds like a motive to me.'

'But… I didn't kill him!'

Angela tried to put herself in the woman's shoes. If she really had nothing to do with her husband's death, surely she'd throw her and Achim out and report them to the police? But Alexa was doing nothing of the sort. Instead she seemed to be weighing things up. Then she said, 'Let's assume Philipp really was murdered—'

'Yes?'

'I could tell you who it was.'

Angela knew that to accuse someone else was a classic

killer's tactic. But she was keen to hear what Alexa von Baugenwitz had to say. 'Who?'

'That letter Philipp scrawled just before he died—'

'Yes.'

'I know who it stands for.'

'Who?'

'Someone who has a far greater motive for murder than me.'

'And who is this someone?'

Alexa hesitated.

'Aren't you going to tell us?'

'She's dangerous… She won't shy away from anything,' said Alexa, shuddering.

Angela wasn't sure if her fear was genuine or not.

'I'll protect you,' said Achim, but this offer didn't seem to help. The opposite, in fact.

'The police will help,' said Angela, trying to sound reassuring. She was desperate for Alexa to reveal the secret of the 'a' – assuming she wasn't lying.

'That inspector is a total loser.'

Angela couldn't deny this. 'I'll give you my body-guard,' she said.

Alexa seemed on the point of accepting when Wood called from the other side of the door.

'Honey, I'm freezing my ass off out here. I'm coming in.'

Alexa looked at Angela. 'You have to go now. Let's speak tomorrow morning. Away from anyone else.'

'When and where?'

'The church opens at six in the morning. Let's meet beside the altar just after that. Now, go!'

Angela and Achim hurried back along the secret passage. As she climbed back up the metal rungs, Angela thought: Either Alexa's telling the truth and she really is terrified of the mysterious 'α' or the meeting in the church is a trap!

28

When Angela and Achim turned into their street at around two in the morning, all the small timber-frame houses were in darkness apart from one. And outside it stood Mike, like a father waiting for his son at night. A son who ought to have been home hours ago, was doubtless drunk, and might well have written off the credit-financed family SUV.

'Mike doesn't look happy,' noted Achim.

'No.' Angela felt a twinge of guilt at having gone behind her bodyguard's back.

'I feel like turning around,' said Achim.

'Look, he's hardly going to lay into us. I'm his boss.'

'I wouldn't be so sure.'

By now they were close enough to see just how grim the expression on Mike's face was.

For a brief moment Angela fancied she could see steam issuing from his ears, but it was just the glow of the kitchen light through the window.

'Where have you been?' said Mike in a tone of restrained rage. It was obvious that he wanted to yell the words at top volume.

'Well,' Achim began, 'it is hard to give a philosophical

or scientific answer this question – for example in relation to the rotation of the earth – since—'

The blood vessels in Mike's head seemed to swell and his Adam's apple twitched.

Achim took half a step behind his wife. 'I'll let your boss answer.'

For the second time that evening, Angela opted to go on the offensive. 'We broke into the castle,' she said.

'You did WHAT?' Now Mike *was* yelling.

'We broke into the castle,' Achim repeated helpfully.

'I heard! I just can't believe it! What if you'd been caught?'

'We were.'

Sometimes Angela wished Achim would keep his mouth shut.

'By who?'

'Alexa von Baugenwitz,' said Angela.

'And an almost naked Texan,' added Achim.

'Naked...?' Mike seemed to be short-circuiting. 'This job was supposed to be good for my nerves!'

'Nothing happened, though,' said Angela reassuringly.

'Precisely,' said Achim. 'The Texan was about to hit Angela with the champagne bottle, but—'

Mike clutched his head. 'How many times have I told you that you're not allowed out on your own! I can't do my job if you sneak around behind my back!' He looked Angela directly in the eye. 'I resign!'

These words hit Angela harder than any resignation tendered by a minister. To be honest, the prospect of not seeing most of her cabinet colleagues again had secretly

137

thrilled her. Only now did she realise how fond she had become of Mike. On no account must he be allowed to resign!

'It won't happen again,' she promised, full of genuine remorse.

'You said that earlier. You even *swore* it!'

'I had my fingers crossed behind my back.' Angela felt guiltier than ever. At any moment Mike might be required to sacrifice his life for her, and she had thanked him by fibbing like a small child.

'*What?*' It was hard to tell whether the bodyguard was more hurt or angry.

'She had her fingers—'

'I'M NOT DEAF!' roared Mike. Achim took a step back. Now Angela felt worse still because her husband was on the receiving end of the anger that she herself deserved. But before she could offer any further explanation, a voice shouted from the house opposite, 'Oi! Turn it down, or I'll call the police!'

'We should go inside,' Angela said to Mike.

'Yes,' he said coldly. 'I've got to pack my suitcase anyway.'

'Mike, I need you!'

'Clearly not.'

'Let's chat about this calmly,' Angela implored as they entered the house.

'It's too late.'

'I've still got three of those vanilla cupcakes...'

'Perhaps the suitcase can wait...'

They went into the kitchen. Angela put the cupcakes on the table and Achim opened a bottle of homemade apricot schnapps, although he poured a glass for himself only. He knew from experience that nobody who sampled this pungent concoction ever came back for more.

'I'm deeply, deeply sorry,' Angela told Mike, 'to have caused you such worry.'

'Who says I was worried?'

'I beg you not to resign.'

Mike didn't reply, and Angela scented one last chance: she had to appeal to his sense of professional honour. 'I need protection early tomorrow morning. There's no way I can find a new bodyguard by then. Surely you don't want to let me go out alone, potentially risking my life again?'

'Your life?' Mike's sulky expression was replaced by a look of alarm.

'It's possible that Alexa von Baugenwitz is setting a trap for us.'

'A trap?' said Achim, refilling his shot glass.

'I think it's highly likely. She's inheriting the castle. She's not showing the slightest grief for her dead husband. Instead, the very next night, she's sleeping with another man – the very man she's sold the castle to.'

'Yes,' Achim said. 'You could call her a merry widow.'

'More like a black widow.'

'Surely she'd never dare lay a finger on someone like you.'

'Not just me – us! We're the only two people who know about her relationship. The only ones on her case.'

'No, I can't believe any woman would take such a risk, however cold-blooded she is.'

'What if she's a psychopath?'

'Do you think she is?'

'As I said, she's showing no sign of grief. And hopping into bed with a Texan the night after the baron's death.'

'That does sound a bit like a psychopath,' Achim said, a shiver running down his spine.

Angela turned to her bodyguard. 'And that's why I need you,' she said.

'Should I request back-up?' asked Mike.

Angela knew this would be the sensible move. She could pick up the phone herself and call the head of the federal police, who would send entire units for her protection. But that wasn't what she wanted. She was determined to solve the case on her own, like a true detective. She knew the thrill it would give her if, on top of her achievements in science and politics, she succeeded as a sleuth too. More importantly, the people of Klein-Freudenstadt would no longer just see her as a has-been ex-chancellor, but a valued member of the community who'd made the village a safer place to live. And then they would welcome Angela with open arms.

'I think you'll be able to deal with a woman,' she said to Mike.

'Perhaps in my job,' Mike sighed. 'But not the ones in my personal life.'

'That's decided then. No need to call for back-up.'

'This job is terrible for my nerves.'

'Eat a cupcake, that'll calm you down,' Angela said, nudging one his way. The bodyguard didn't need a second invitation. She was delighted that Mike wasn't going to resign anymore. And she was very excited about the

140

next day. If Alexa set a trap, it would prove that she was the killer. Then Mike would take her by surprise and the whole episode would turn into a trap for the black widow herself!

29

It was a beautiful morning.

Was it also a deadly morning?

The sun rose picturesquely above Klein-Freuden-stadt's deserted market square, dousing the church tower in a blood-red light. The air was thick with the aroma of freshly baked rolls from the nearby bakery, which went by the curious name of Bäckerei Wurst. Despite last night's ingestion of cupcakes, Mike said, 'That smell is making me hungry.'

'Personally I could do with another schnapps,' said Achim, eyeing the church apprehensively.

'If you manage a third glass of that stuff without sustaining second-degree burns to your oesophagus,' remarked Angela, 'then you're a medical miracle.'

In other circumstances Achim might have laughed at this witticism, but now he was too scared to force a smile. Mike also appeared nervous and kept checking that his pistol was sitting correctly in the holster. Angela was the only one of the little troop who seemed positive. Yes, the situation was potentially dangerous. But stimulating too. Exciting. Exhilarating even. They were about to arrest a murderer. This was of a quite different order from delivering the closing address at a G7 summit!

Only Putin was in exactly the same mood as usual as he trotted between them on the cobbles of the market square. Angela had wanted to leave the dog at home, but he'd done such an egregious fart that she feared another flokati mishap.

Had Wurst the baker or anyone else been out and about to observe them, the four figures with the rising sun at their backs would have looked like a racing team out of a *Fast and Furious* film. They weren't actually walking in slow motion, but the closer they got to the church, the slacker their pace became.

'It's not too late to turn around,' said Achim.

'Nothing is going to happen to us,' said Angela.

'Famous last words,' said Mike, reeling off his favourite phrase.

'What exactly do you mean by that?' said Achim.

'Let's discuss it later,' said Angela, trying to prevent her husband's nervousness from infecting the whole group.

'I only hope,' said Mike, 'that your plan works.'

'It will definitely succeed,' declared Angela in her most authoritative tone of voice, partly to dispel the faint doubts bubbling up inside her too.

'Famous last words,' muttered Mike again.

With an effort Angela ignored him. 'Let's run through the plan one last time,' she said. 'I go up to the altar, where Alexa von Baugenwitz is waiting for me.'

'While I,' said Achim, his voice a little unsteady, 'will remain by the door. And at the moment when the woman confesses to her crime—'

'But before she has time to pull out a gun—'

142

'I wrench open the door—'

'At which point,' said Mike, 'I enter with my pistol at the ready.'

'Exactly!' said Angela.

It was a simple plan, and a welcome change from those she'd had to devise as a politician, when there had always been hundreds of variables and thousands of possible outcomes to consider. There had been things you knew, things you didn't know, things you knew you didn't know, and things you didn't know you didn't know. And all of them could kick you up the backside.

How refreshing it was to be able to think in a straight line from A to B without any other letters getting in the way – let alone an entire Sumerian alphabet laced with Chinese pictograms converted by a madman into a DIY version of Morse code.

Putin raised his head and barked. He seemed to be looking up at the church tower.

'Is someone up there?' said Mike, his hand moving nervously towards his holster.

'Probably a crow.'

'What if the black widow has back-up?' said Achim. 'The naked Texan, for example.'

'I don't want to think about naked Texans,' said Mike.

'Understandable.'

Angela decided to intervene with a dose of her famous logic. 'If Alexa does pull a gun on us,' she explained, 'it means she's a psychopath. But since the Texan is definitely not a psychopath, he won't help her.'

'He's planning to fly to Mars!' said Achim.

'Yes, but that's just part and parcel of being a Silicon Valley billionaire.'

Mike turned to Achim. 'What if Alexa pulls out a gun quicker than you can open the door?'

'Don't worry about that. I can always depend on my Achim,' said Angela, whose trust mitigated some of her husband's nervousness.

They were now standing right outside the church, Angela on the *Stone of Tears* that the inhabitants of Klein-Freudenstadt had dedicated to Adelheid von Baugenwitz after she freed the village from the tyranny of her husband Balduin and leapt to her death. Angela took a deep breath in and out – Mike and Achim followed suit – then pushed down the handle. The door opened, just as Alexa had said it would. Yet Angela hesitated to enter. Although she felt euphoric at the prospect of arresting a killer, she was also aware she'd never been in such danger before. Not even on her flights to Afghanistan. Or when Silvio Berlusconi tried to embrace her. On the other hand they had to apprehend the murderer before she could kill again. Just as she was about to thrust open the door Putin barked once more.

Angela stopped.

'Woof! Woof! Woof!'

They all looked up to the tower.

'Uh-oh,' said Achim.

'Shit!' said Mike.

Standing on the balustrade of the belltower was Alexa von Baugenwitz.

Until she wasn't standing there anymore.

144

But falling.

Mike pushed Achim, Angela and Putin to one side and shielded them all on the ground with his huge body.

Alexa von Baugenwitz came crashing down less than half a metre away.

Flat bang on the *Stone of Tears*.

30

Angela's head was a tangle of thoughts.

'Oh God, she's killed herself.'

'Oh God, she almost fell on Achim and killed him.'

'Better for me to die than Achim.'

'Wow, Mike's heavy.'

'Perhaps he shouldn't eat so much cake.'

'Or at least cut out the cream.'

'Strange what goes through your mind when adrenaline is pumping around your body.'

'Ahem,' wheezed Achim, his thin body almost crushed by the colossus that was Mike, 'please could you get up now?'

'Only when the coast is clear.'

'How do you expect to establish that when you're lying on top of us?'

'Good point,' Mike said, springing to his feet and whipping the pistol from its holster.

Angela and Achim stood up too, albeit not quite as athletically. Before Angela could look over at the dead Alexa von Baugenwitz, Achim placed his hands over her eyes.

'Why are you doing that?' she asked.

'It's too horrible a sight for you.'

'Yesterday we all watched a body being cut open. I wasn't the one who felt unwell.'

Mike was making every effort to avoid looking at the body. He was already a touch pale around the nose, but seemed to be in control of the situation. He put his pistol back in its holster, a sign that all appeared to be clear.

Only now did Angela see that her husband was shaking. She took his hand, then looked over at Alexa's body. Had she leapt to her death out of guilt, like the wife of the seventeenth-century butcher Balduin may have done? Over the years Angela had come to the conclusion that history didn't repeat itself. Usually history came up with something new, something that had never happened before, as if to mock the smartest historians with their impotence. But here in Klein-Freudenstadt history really did seem to be repeating itself: a woman murdering her unfaithful husband then jumping from the church tower.

Such were Angela's thoughts for exactly forty-three seconds, during which time Achim regained his composure and Mike avoided looking at the corpse. In the forty-fourth second, however, Putin began to bark.

'What's up?' said Angela.

'Putin can't talk,' said Achim.

'Shh! He heard something.'

The three strained to listen but Putin started barking even louder. 'And you can shh too!' Angela told him.

The pug looked at her. For a moment Angela thought that he was reacting to her natural authority just as the officials in the chancellery used to. But then he simply went on barking. She fished a dog biscuit from her blazer pocket to shut him up.

Footsteps.

She heard footsteps!

Inside the church!

'Somebody's in there,' Mike said, grabbing his pistol again.

Whoever is inside the church could have pushed Alexa! thought Angela, squeezing Achim's hand more tightly.

'I'm going in,' whispered Mike, opening the door with caution.

Angela was about to whisper back, 'Me too,' but as she opened her mouth Mike hissed, 'Don't even think about it!'

Mike entered the church. After a few paces he shouted, 'Hey, stop right there!'

Angela felt sure that inside the church was a killer. And no matter what Mike said, she had to go in. Yes, a great detective preferred to unmask a murderer through brilliant deduction, but sometimes the killer was simply caught in the act. Besides, given how woefully wide of the mark all her deliberations had been so far, this was the best chance she had of solving the case.

Angela let go of Achim's hand and left him with a disappointed Putin, who'd been hoping for more treats. As she peered into the dark interior of the church, she saw Mike heading for the altar. She could also just about make out a figure fleeing towards the side exit. The person was dressed all in black with a black hood. A phantom!

The black figure was soon out of the church, the door crashing shut again. Mike ran up and shook the handle but it wouldn't open. He kicked the wood, again in vain.

'Let's run around the outside of the church and try to catch him,' said Angela to Achim, scuttling off as fast as she could. Behind her she heard Achim sighing as he got into gear, 'For better, for worse—'

No sooner had the two of them turned the corner than they saw a figure in black, just a few metres away, in the shadow cast by the church wall.

'It's heading straight for us,' said Achim.

'Yes.' For the first time Angela was really frightened. She wanted to run back but knew that she'd be too slow to give the phantom the slip. Achim probably wouldn't make it either, even though he was quicker than she was. She couldn't bear the thought that she'd be responsible for his death!

Putin barked behind her. Would he be her salvation? But instead of attacking the figure, the dog barked at Angela's coat pocket. He was demanding more biscuits!

Suddenly a shot rang out.

'Goodness gracious!' exclaimed Achim.

'Bloody hell!' exclaimed Angela, wondering as she did so if there was anyone alive apart from her husband who could say 'goodness gracious' in a situation like this.

'Help!' cried the hooded figure. It had a deep voice, certainly not female and with no hint of a Texan accent.

'DO NOT MOVE!' commanded Mike, who'd dashed out of the church and fired the warning shot with his pistol. The figure, its face still in shadow, was rooted to

148

the spot. It raised its hands. 'Please don't shoot!'

'Give me one good reason why I shouldn't.'

'Because I've just wet myself.'

'What kind of reason is that?'

'I'll give you all the valuable items from the church!'

'What?' said Mike.

'Take the collection too. It's meant to be for Bread for the World, but—'

Mike was too confused to speak. Unlike Angela, who had realised that the man before them wasn't the phantom they'd seen in the church but somebody quite different. 'Are you the pastor?' she asked.

'Yes, who else did you think I was?'

'We thought you were the killer of Alexa von Baugenwitz,' said Angela unhappily. 'But whoever she is, she's now long gone.'

31

'Murder? Are you serious?' said Inspector Hannemann, slouching on a church pew. Along with Angela, Achim, Mike and Putin, he was waiting inside the church while the body of Alexa von Baugenwitz was taken away. There were no bystanders as it was still early in the day, but it was better for all concerned for Angela to remain out of sight, just in case any reporters turned up.

'Yes, murder,' said Angela. 'We glimpsed the suspect, but weren't able to identify her. She ran out of the church.'

Hannemann sighed for perhaps the tenth time that morning.

'Is that all you can do? Sigh?'

'Yes, when I have to listen to your gory fantasies.'

'Hey! Please talk to my wife with the respect she deserves!' said Achim angrily from near the altar. He had taken the opportunity to inspect the stained-glass window. It depicted saints: killing dragons, talking to animals or simply gazing up at the sky.

Hannemann ignored him. 'This is what happened: your bodyguard accosted the pastor in the church. He got a fright, left through the side door and ran away.'

'The figure in the church was definitely not the pastor,' said Mike. 'I'm sure of it.'

'Why don't you ask him yourself?' said Angela. 'He can confirm he wasn't in the church.'

'I can't. He's having a shower and getting changed – he was pretty whiffy.'

Talk about the pot calling the kettle black, thought Angela. The inspector honked like Horst Seemann at the end of a long night of coalition negotiations.

'Anyway,' Hannemann said, standing up, 'I have to go. I've got an appointment with my divorce lawyer.'

'That's more important than a murder?'

'If I don't get a divorce soon, I might commit a murder myself.'

Hannemann got to the end of the pew but Angela blocked his way. 'Those sorts of appointments can be moved,' she said.

'Not when your lawyer is about to fly to Mallorca for six weeks.'

'It is unacceptable to put your private life before your

duty.' Angela was outraged. Not once had she ditched a work commitment in favour of a personal one! She remembered the evening of her sixty-sixth birthday, which she'd spent thrashing out an EU budget deal with Emmanuel Macron and Giuseppe Conte even though she'd far rather have been enjoying a couple of glasses of champagne in the Brussels hotel bar with Achim. Still, the drudgery had been somewhat sweetened by the bouquet of sixty-six roses that the French president and Italian prime minister had surprised her with.

'If this were actually important,' said Hannemann, 'I might agree with you.'

'A murder is important!'

'Certainly. This, however, was suicide. As was Philipp von Baugenwitz's death.'

'Two suicides in such a short period of time. Doesn't that seem a bit fishy to you?'

'Listen, I can understand you're getting a bit bored in retirement,' said Hannemann patronisingly.

'I'm sorry?' Angela thought she'd misheard.

'It can't be easy, having to cope with not being important anymore. With the fact that nobody's interested in you now you've lost your status.'

Angela couldn't believe what she was hearing.

'When our mayor in Klein-Freudenstadt retired after twenty years,' continued Hannemann, 'he too was confronted by the brutal truth: people had only ever been nice to him because they wanted something. That hit him hard. But did he go around inventing murder cases…?'

'I'm not inventing murder cases!'

'No, he didn't. Instead he took up a hobby. He's a bird-watcher now. They're much nicer than people, he finds. You should have a go at it too.'

'I'm not going to watch any birds.'

'We've got a lot of frogs around here too.'

'Nor frogs.'

'Trees? You can even hug those.'

Angela felt like giving him a good clip round the ear. She was used to such rudeness from men like Trump, Orban and Putin, but not from little clowns like Hanne-mann, who only dared to be so disrespectful because she no longer enjoyed the authority of her office.

'Whatever,' said Hannemann. He squeezed past her, 'First I'm off to see my lawyer. And then I'll fill out the report for the suicide.'

'How often do I have to tell you this wasn't a suicide?'

'I'm not going to listen to any more nonsense! Par-ticularly not from an old biddy who doesn't know what to do with her time!'

In her head, she gave the inspector an almighty slap. In real life Angela held back and strove to be construc-tive. 'Would you at least question the pastor again?'

'Sure, sure, if there's time,' the inspector said as he made his way out. He might as well have said, 'I'll set up a working group.' Angela knew it was pointless to expect anything from this man.

'Shall I give him a good hiding?' asked Mike.

Angela would have liked nothing more, but she knew it wasn't a solution. She merely shook her head as Han-nemann left the church.

'I can't tell you how often I've wanted to give that man a good smack!'

It was a woman's voice. They all turned to the side door through which the black figure had fled just half an hour earlier. Now it was open again and Lena, in police uniform, had come in.

'You got the door open,' said Angela.

'The key was in the lock on the other side,' said Lena, shooting Mike a friendly smile and receiving an uncertain yet at the same time besotted one in return.

At least two of us can smile, thought Angela. She now felt more furious with herself than with Hannemann. If only her detective work were better she wouldn't have had to take any abuse from that joker.

'We should get out of here,' said Lena. 'The reporter from the local paper is here and you should make yourselves scarce before he sees you. Let's use the side entrance.'

'Good plan,' said Achim. He grabbed Putin, who was sniffing suspiciously at a statue of Jesus.

Mike went up to Lena. 'There's definitely no one behind the church?' he asked.

'No, you'll be able to slip away unnoticed.'

'Excellent.'

'Are you free again this evening?' said Lena.

The question seemed to catch Mike off-guard. 'Yes, I think so.'

'Let's go for a swim, then. In the lake.'

Mike instinctively glanced at his tummy.

Lena tapped it with a finger. 'Swimming's a great way to lose a few grams.'

'But I... I don't have any trunks.'

'You won't need them.'

The policewoman was enjoying watching the big man blush.

'Remember skinny dipping?' said Achim to Angela. 'We used to do that all the time in the GDR.'

Lena and Mike stared at the elder couple open-mouthed, their minds working overtime to suppress the images conjured by these words.

'Shall we keep to the matter in hand?' said Angela, receiving a vigorous nod from the pair.

As the group made their way out of the church, Angela took a closer look at the door. The crack Mike had made trying to kick it open looked almost identical to the one in the door to the castle dungeon. She had a hunch this might be a clue as to why the door to the wine cellar had been locked from the inside. She was determined to solve the puzzle that very day, and to do this she had to become a grittier detective. Only then would she be able to expose the killer. It was clear that whoever it was must have a degree of sophistication. After all, she had managed to make Philipp's murder look like a suicide. Even more impressively, she had contrived to make Alexa von Baugenwitz's death seem like a repeat of the incident from the seventeenth century.

Angela was going to show the inspector – and not just him but the whole world – that she was still useful, even in retirement!

Most of all, though, she wanted to prove it to herself.

'Could you slow down a little?' begged Achim.

'I can't,' said Angela, as she marched towards the castle, lit by the morning sun.

'Putin's getting really heavy!'

'Give him to Mike.'

Mike glanced at the slobbering pug. 'Not in my job description,' he said.

'You're just worried he'll ruin your jacket,' said Achim.

'And your point is?'

'As far as I'm concerned, both of you can go back home,' said Angela irritably.

'I'm not permitted to leave you alone,' said Mike.

'And I shouldn't either... given your state of mind,' added Achim.

'What exactly is that supposed to mean?' Angela was feeling more and more cross.

'Nothing, nothing,' said Achim hastily. When his wife was in full flow you could rapidly become collateral damage.

'We are now playing hardball, as the Americans like to say,' declared Angela.

'Oh dear,' groaned Achim.

'What do you mean by that?'

Achim hesitated.

'I asked you a question!'

'When you're worked up like this you're only successful 23.8 per cent of the time.'

Despite her scientific training, Angela ignored him. 'I'm going to give Katharina von Baugenwitz a good talking-to,' she said, striding towards the main entrance.

Mike stood in her way. 'You're putting yourself in more and more danger. Look, we know now that there really is a killer, whatever that fool of an inspector thinks. I'm going to call for back-up.'

'No, you are not!' said Angela as Mike fished out his mobile. 'I do not want any more guard dogs.'

'But—'

'If you make that call, I will make one myself and have you transferred.'

This hit home.

'With immediate effect, before your date with Lena.'

'But it's my duty!'

'You are obliged to follow my instructions!'

Mike stepped aside. 'I am,' he said bitterly.

'That was a bit harsh,' whispered Achim to his wife.

Angela knew he was right. She had been unfair. This good, honest man was just trying to do his job. But she was on too much of a roll to apologise now. She would do so later – once she'd brought to book Katharina von Baugenwitz, who she now regarded as the chief suspect. There had to be something dodgy about her alibi. The woman had more reason than anyone to hate Philipp and Alexa. Besides, the history of the von Baugenwitz family meant more to her than to anyone else on the planet. Wasn't it logical that she would be inspired to imitate the deaths of Adelheid and Balduin?

'When you're in this mood,' said Achim, 'your chances of success sink to 17.1 per cent.'

'Shut up, Achim.'

'13.5 per cent now that you've started to have a go at me.'

Angela took a deep breath. Achim was right. She would have to apologise to him too. Later. As she looked away her eyes fell on a red Tesla; it must be the Texan investor's car. He was probably still asleep. At any rate, he wasn't a suspect. He wouldn't be able to buy the castle now that Alexa was dead. She could probably rule out a crime of passion too; the internet had informed her that he changed his women as often as Britain did its prime ministers.

'What are you doing here again?' Katharina von Baugenwitz was storming towards them from the castle. 'Is nobody's grief sacred to you lot?'

Angela doubted that Katharina was grieving very much. Firmly and directly, just as she'd resolved to be, she asked her, 'Where were you at six o'clock this morning?'

'What?'

'You heard what I said!'

Behind his wife, Achim said quietly, '7.9 per cent.'

'Who do you think you are, talking to me like this?' hissed Katharina.

'Why won't you answer? Do you have something to hide?'

'There have been two suicides here. I am in mourning. And you're treating me like a criminal!'

'They weren't suicides,' said Angela. 'We saw someone in the church dressed head to toe in black. We could only just make them out, but it's plain that whoever it was pushed Alexa from the roof!'

Katharina turned white.

'So, where were you at six o'clock this morning?'

The manager was reeling. 'If I tell you will you leave me alone?'

'If I find your answer convincing.'

'I was with Angela Kessler.'

'What were you talking about so early in the morning?'

'She's a farmer – she gets up at four. I needed to speak to her because she's behind on her lease.'

'You mean she owes the castle estate money?'

'I'm sorry… I'm really not up to talking about it right now.' Katharina turned away. The woman was ashen-faced. As she had been yesterday when Angela quizzed her and Alexa about the 'ɑ'. Since then one of the two women had been killed, while the other had an alibi for the night when Philipp died, and now claimed to have one for the second murder too. Maybe not everything supported the theory that Katharina was the killer. Still, Angela wasn't simply going to let the woman go. She would have to be tenacious in her usual, rational way – and so lift her chance of success back to 81.4 per cent. She pointed at the 'ɑ' she'd drawn in the gravel yesterday and said, 'You know what Philipp meant by this.'

It was astonishing how much colour could drain from a face that was already so pale.

'Who is it?' Angela pressed her.

'I… I don't know what you're talking about. Listen, I don't feel well, I need a lie down.' Katharina turned and almost ran back into the castle.

She may not be the killer, thought Angela, but she certainly knows something.

'That was all a show,' said Achim. 'She's the killer, no doubt about it.'

'Well, it's quite simple to check. Do you know what we're going to do now?'

'Go home so I can finally put Putin down?' said Achim.

'Retreat to a place of safety?' said Mike.

'Neither of those.'

'Why doesn't that surprise me?' sighed the bodyguard, channelling Inspector Hannemann.

'My wife is full of surprises,' said Achim, not without a hint of pride.

'But – I said she *didn't* surprise me.'

Angela ignored them. 'We're going to pay a visit to a certain farmer,' she declared.

33

Angela and Mike strode across one of the many fields on the castle's estate. Achim had returned home to give Putin his breakfast. Even a pug couldn't live on treats alone.

'Why do bodyguards always have to be dressed in black?' said Mike. He was sweating in the summer heat.

'Gaddafi's female bodyguards went around with bare midriffs,' said Angela.

'You won't catch me doing that.'

'Oh, come on, I'm sure Lena would enjoy the view.'

Mike turned red.

'You could even get her a matching outfit.'

Mike reddened further.

Angela was having a whale of a time but she decided not to push it too far. Maybe later. So she just said, 'You're going to have to get used to it. We women from the east like to take the initiative.'

Mike's face was now a study in scarlet. In other circumstances Angela might have conducted an experiment to see how many further shades of the colour she could induce. But duty first: she was here to interrogate the other Angela, who was on her tractor ploughing the field fifty metres away.

'Hello!' she shouted over the engine noise, stepping onto the field and waving. The woman didn't wave back or offer any kind of greeting. The tractor was heading straight for Angela with no signs of slowing down.

'Watch out! She's going to run you over!' said Mike, adopting a combat position.

'Not going to happen.'

'Famous last words.'

'I'd be grateful if you refrained from saying that in my presence.'

The tractor drew ever closer, but the farmer made no move to slow down. Not even when she was ten metres away. But Angela refused to give her the satisfaction of jumping out of the way. She stood there steadfast on the field, reminiscent of Gary Cooper in the classic Western *High Noon*, had Gary Cooper been dressed in black cloth trousers and a magenta blazer.

Angela could see the whites of the farmer's crazed eyes, her grimace of disgust… She herself assumed a poker face reminiscent of Doc Holliday in the classic

Western *Gunfight at the O.K. Corral*, had Doc Holliday formed a diamond with his hands to ground him while playing poker.

The tractor was only a few metres away. Mike grasped his pistol. Any second now he would whip it out and jump in front of the tractor. Little as she desired this to happen, Angela was determined to show no weakness.

The two women were now locked in a staring duel, which made Angela think of Burt Lancaster before the shootout in *Gunfight at the O.K. Corral*.

And like Burt Lancaster, Angela won her duel, only without an exchange of fire. The farmer brought the tractor to a stop just in front of her. She was furious at being forced to interrupt her ploughing, but even more so because she'd lost the staring match.

'What are you doing here?'

'I've come to talk to you.'

'Can't you see I've got work to do?'

'I could sit next to you on the tractor.'

The other Angela looked less than thrilled, but she made no objection.

'I'd have to come too,' said Mike. 'My job is as a bodyguard.'

'You can trot along behind us,' said the farmer.

Angela nodded at Mike and climbed onto the tractor. Before she had seated herself properly, her namesake had started the engine and lurched forward. No doubt she was hoping that Angela would fall off, but with all her experience of perching on camels and elephants on state visits, keeping her balance on a tractor was a doddle.

Breathing in the diesel fumes as he marched along in their wake, Mike muttered to himself, 'This is worse than Baghdad.'

'So,' said the farmer without deigning to look at Angela, 'what do you want?'

'Alexa von Baugenwitz was murdered this morning.'

'Bloody hell!' There was no sorrow in her voice, but the surprise sounded genuine. 'Do they know who did it?'

'That's what I'm trying to find out.'

'You?' Now the farmer did look at Angela, with an incredulous smile.

'Yes, me.'

She laughed scornfully. 'You really do have an inflated opinion of yourself, don't you?'

Angela felt insulted. First she'd had to put up with Inspector Hannemann's condescension, and now this! She would show them both.

'I believe Philipp von Baugenwitz was murdered too.'

'It wouldn't surprise me.'

'No?' For her part Angela *was* surprised. The farmer was the first suspect not to immediately scoff at her murder theory.

'I mean, he's had every woman around here. It's not for nothing that they call him von Beddenblitz.'

'What about you?' asked Angela. The tractor halted so abruptly that Mike almost went into the back of it.

'Get off.'

'I'm assuming that response means "Yes, I did have a relationship with him".' Angela saw no reason to spare the woman's feelings.

'I said get off.'

'Only if you answer one more question.'

'I'll push you off, you know.'

Angela was undeterred. After all, she had Mike to protect her. 'Did you meet Katharina von Baugenwitz this morning?' she said.

'Yes, the stupid bitch came to tell us farmers to stay away from Philipp's funeral.'

This seemed to confirm Katharina's alibi. And also to rule out the possibility that the xenophobic farmer had anything to do with Alexa's murder, no matter how badly the baron had hurt her. Now Angela had all the information she'd come for, so there was no need to stay any longer. But no sooner had she got up from the seat than the other Angela said, 'Do you want to know who killed them both?'

Angela felt like saying, 'No, I was just asking those questions for fun.' But she bit her tongue and asked, 'Who?'

'The black whore.'

'How dare you talk about Marie like that!'

'I'll not mince my words.'

Angela tried to think of a cutting riposte but all she could come up with was, 'They'd make pretty rotten mince.'

'Look, do you want to know the truth, or not?'

'Go on.'

'He dumped me for her.'

'So he did break your heart,' said Angela, clambering down from the tractor. She didn't want to stay in this

163

obnoxious woman's company a moment longer than she had to.

'This isn't about me, it's about her. She didn't use contraception and Philipp wasn't one to use condoms. As soon as she told him she was carrying his child he broke off all contact with her and denied he was the father – and his lawyers made it clear he would never take a paternity test. So he left her to look after herself. Naturally she gets a small fortune in benefits, though it seems even that isn't enough for her given that she tried to kill herself. She couldn't even do that right.'

Angela felt like socking her namesake. In these situations the diamond was the only solution. Thus grounded, she felt her rage subside and gave way to sympathy for Marie. The woman had tried to take her own life, like her own beloved substitute mother. How lonely and desperate she must have been!

'Afterwards,' continued the unpleasant farmer, 'she must have thought about it a bit and realised it was better to kill him. And his wife.'

'I'm not going to listen to these outrageous accusations a moment longer.' Angela began to walk away.

'You know the mistake you do-gooders always make?' the farmer shouted after her.

'That we ever listen to people like you?'

'Political correctness stops you from seeing the truth.' She started the engine, blasting exhaust fumes at Angela and Mike, and chugged off to plough more furrows.

'I don't like to say this,' said Mike when he'd stopped coughing, 'but she may be right.'

164

'What do you mean?'

'Marie does have a motive. After all, she tried to take her own life, which means she must have been so badly hurt she was capable of anything.'

'Don't jump to any hasty conclusions.'

'What's hasty about it? Who else could be the killer? There's nobody left.'

Angela strained to think. It was true that all the suspects apart from Marie had an alibi. So it could only be her. Unless...

'What if the farmer is deliberately putting us on the wrong track to divert attention from herself?'

'But she has an alibi for this morning – she was with Katharina.'

'Hold on a second. Didn't she say that Katharina had come to tell her and the other farmers to stay away from the baron's funeral?'

'So what?' said Mike.

'Katharina told us she needed to talk to Angela about arrears.'

'Maybe she was just too embarrassed to admit she was in debt.'

'It's possible,' said Angela doubtfully. For a while she walked beside Mike, deep in thought. 'What if the pair of them are in cahoots?' she said as they left the field.

'But Katharina has an alibi for the first killing too.'

'From Lena.'

'Exactly.'

'Do you know Agatha Christie's *Murder on the Orient Express*?'

'No, I only watch action films.'

'It's a book too.'

'Nice,' said Mike.

Angela gathered that books weren't his entertainment of choice. 'At the novel's dénouement,' she explained, 'it turns out that all twelve of the suspects committed the murder together.'

'And you really think Lena would be involved in something like that?' Mike reddened again, this time from anger.

'It's possible. The baron ruined her sporting career. Maybe three women ganged up to seek revenge for all the suffering he'd caused them. And then, because Alexa was going to expose them, they got her out of the way too. Hence the fact that they all give each other alibis. What do you think?'

'You want to know what I think?' said Mike in a tone not appropriate when addressing one's boss – although the heat, the fumes and the fact that he was falling in love with one of the suspects may be considered mitigating circumstances.

'What?' asked Angela a little nervously.

'You should stop playing your detective games.'

'That's none of your business.'

'You haven't made any progress whatsoever.'

'I've gathered information.'

'Yes – information that has only led to dumb theories.'

'They're not dumb.'

'*Murder on the Orient Express*!' snorted Mike.

Angela's theory began to sound a bit far-fetched, even

to herself. But the only alternative was that Marie must be the killer. And Angela found this simply impossible to believe. Could her insight into human nature really be so weak?

'I suggest you have a good think about this,' continued Mike. 'Either you stop putting yourself in danger with your play detective work, or I really will resign.'

For Angela this was a blow to the stomach. Never before had a subordinate – at any rate not one she'd cared about – spoken to her like this. Nonetheless, there was no question of giving up now. But nor could she bear to lose Mike… And on one point he was absolutely correct: she had to come up with some results if anyone, herself included, was ever going to take her seriously as a detective.

If there was one thing Angela had learned in politics, it was this: if you weren't making any progress with a problem, you had to think outside the box. For example, ask yourself what the Russian president really wants when he turns up to Syrian peace negotiations, because the answer certainly isn't peace. Or whether one should simply do without summits, given that they always ended badly. Or, since no amount of complaints seemed to improve the food in the chancellery canteen, whether they shouldn't just open an account with Über Eats.

So if she was getting nowhere with the question 'Who is the killer?' why not ask 'How did she do it?'

'How about you give me until midday?' she said.

'Then what?'

'If I haven't got anywhere by then, I'll quit.'

'Agreed.'

Mike's relief was obvious. Clearly he was certain that Angela would make no progress.

'Come on then,' said Angela. She set off decisively, while in the background the other Angela kept on ploughing. Yet the former chancellor felt gripped by uncertainty. Would she really be able to solve the mystery of the baron's murder within a few hours? Or would she have to admit that she was just a ordinary pensioner who ought to have stuck to baking cakes.

34

For the second time that morning, Angela and Mike entered the castle courtyard. On this occasion they were not intercepted by an irate Katharina, nor was the Texan's red Tesla anywhere to be seen. There was just Pia, sitting by the fountain, wearing sunglasses and holding a paper cup in her right hand. The aroma of coffee drifted over. Mingled with something else.

'Smells like weed,' said Mike.

'It reminds me of the Bundestag,' said Angela.

'The Greens?'

'All parties, actually.'

The pair wandered over to the blue-haired teenager. She took a final toke from her joint then tossed it over her shoulder into the fountain.

'Those fish are going to be pretty chilled,' said Mike under his breath.

Pia looked at them without making any move to get

up, took another sip of coffee and said in bored tone, 'I suppose you've come to offer your condolences, just for a change?'

'Would you like to hear them?' asked Angela.

'I never liked Alexa.'

'Is there anyone you do like?'

'Here or anywhere else in the world?'

'Let's start with here.'

'No.'

'Anywhere else?'

'No.'

'You're a right little ray of sunshine, aren't you?' said Mike.

'My fans like the way I am.'

'She's an influencer,' said Angela, seeing Mike's confusion.

'Does she sell bad moods?'

'Hey boomers, didn't anyone tell you it's rude to talk about someone in their presence in the third person?'

'You're right. Sorry,' said Angela.

Pia took another sip.

'Now you can say something like, "That's alright".'

'Are you trying to educate me? A waste of time, as plenty before you can testify.'

Angela decided to change the subject. Pointing to where the Tesla had stood only a couple of hours earlier, she asked, 'Is the American coming back?'

'As soon as he heard about Alexa's death he made a dash for the airport. I bet he's now in his private jet over the Atlantic.'

It made sense that the investor had done a runner.

The last thing he'd want was any media coverage. Death was never good for share prices.

'Is your mother here?'

'She's gone to Templin to pick up the notary from the train station.'

Angela hadn't yet considered the question of who would now inherit the property. Alexa had inherited everything from the baron – that much was clear. But now who would inherit the castle from her? It had to be one of Alexa's relatives. But none of the people left on Angela's list of suspects were related to her. And surely none of them was suddenly going to turn out to be a long-lost sister, aunt or mother? That sort of thing only happened in the South American soap operas that Ursula von der Leyen watched to unwind. So either Angela had been wrong the whole time and the killer was some relative of Alexa who would appear from nowhere, or the murders had been prompted by something other than the inheritance. Like revenge. After all there were more than enough suspects with this motive. Perhaps they really had joined forces to cover each other's backs. Compared to the long-lost-relative-South-American-drama-series theory, the everyone-is-guilty-*Murder-on-the-Orient-Express* one sounded almost plausible.

'Do you know who will inherit the castle from Alexa?' she asked.

'Well, I doubt it's going to be me.'

Angela was surprised that the girl had even mentioned the possibility. Until then nobody had hinted that Pia might benefit from the deaths. As Philipp's ex-stepdaughter she had no claim to the inheritance. And she'd never been close to Alexa von Baugenwitz.

'When did you hear about Alexa's murder?'

'Why don't you just come out with it?'

'What do you mean?' asked Angela, who knew very well what the girl meant.

'You want to know if I've got an alibi. Like yesterday when you wanted to know if I had one for Philip's death.'

'Do you?'

Pia got to her feet, took a last sip of coffee from her cup and threw it into the fountain to join the spliff.

'Hey! Take that back out!' said Mike.

'We've got people for that.'

'Those poor fish!' Mike rolled up the sleeves of his jacket and shirt to pick out the cup and, while he was at it, the joint too.

'Like I said, we've got people for that,' said Pia. Mike glared at her but his boss refused to be distracted. 'We were talking about your alibi.'

'We were.'

'And?'

'I don't have one.'

Angela was taken aback, particularly as Pia accompanied her answer with an insolent grin. 'So, where were you?' she asked.

'It was practically the middle of the night. I was asleep.'

It was plausible. Even as a teenager Angela herself had never had a problem getting up early, but she remembered this hadn't been the case with her school-friends. Despite her regular attempts to encourage them with her

171

'The early bird catches the good grades' motto. All the same, no alibi was no alibi, however plausible.

'And before you ask,' said Pia, 'sleep is not something I make a live feed of. No matter how much my male fans beg me to.'

Angela looked at the girl. It only made sense to suspect her if she was involved in a plot with other suspects. But why should she be? Okay, she'd loathed her former stepfather. But if Pia killed everyone she didn't like she'd soon be the only person left on Earth. And then there was the question of why the other women would rope in a teenage girl to avenge their own broken hearts. Pia wasn't providing them with an alibi. No, the *Murder on the Orient Express* theory was crazy enough with three conspirators. A fourth would push it beyond the bounds of credibility.

Angela had hit another brick wall in the 'whodunnit?' question, so she decided to revert to her original plan and investigate *how* it was done.

'Do you think you could let us into the wine cellar?' she asked.

'Are we going to get smashed? I'm in.'

'You're far too young to be drinking in the morning,' said Mike, dropping the wet joint into the wet paper cup.

'Do I look like the sort of person who's going to listen to that sort of bullshit?'

Mike had to concede that she didn't.

'We don't want to go down to the wine cellar in order to get drunk,' said Angela.

'Shame. What, then?'

'We want to find out how a potential killer might have committed the murder.'

'You really have bugger all to do now you're retired, don't you?'

Angela was getting used to people not taking her investigation seriously. All her life she had been under-estimated – for example after Helmut Kohl resigned – and it had always helped her. So why not in her new role as a detective too? After all, nobody had taken Inspector Columbo or Miss Marple seriously and this had worked to their advantage.

'So, will you let us in?' she asked.

'Whatever... I've got nothing to do today anyhow,' said Pia, making for the castle entrance. Angela and her bodyguard followed.

'I thought you were working as an influencer,' said Mike.

'One hour a day.'

'One hour? That's not work.'

'What do you earn?'

'None of your business.'

'I make 40k a month.'

Mike looked almost as ill as he had during the post-mortem.

'The value of an individual,' observed Angela as they entered the cool, musty hallway, 'isn't measured in gold.'

'Yeah, right,' said Pia.

Rather than pursue the matter further, Angela decided instead to concentrate on the interior of the castle. She saw again the gallery of ancestors. The portraits of Balduin the Butcher and Walter, whose face had been disfigured by a musket shot. Of particular interest to Angela was the painting of Ferdinand von Baugenwitz, who reminded her of Franz von Papen, the last chancellor of the Weimar Republic and the man who paved the way for Hitler. She remembered that if Ferdinand hadn't collaborated with the Nazis his descendants would now have a restitution claim for items worth 200 million euros. And that Katharina had wanted to pursue this claim in court while she was still married to Philipp.

When they turned into the corridor where the dusty bust of General Hindenburg stood, Mike was finally able to discard the soggy cup and its contents into a bin. Rolling down his sleeves, he shook his head. 'Forty grand!'

'In a good month it can be as much as seventy,' said Pia. She didn't sound boastful or provocative – more like an accountant going through the books.

'Crazy,' said Mike. 'Totally crazy.'

'No, it's perfectly logical. I generate revenue for the advertising industry and I get paid for it. They call it attention economics.'

Angela kept out of the conversation. It wasn't as though she would be able to instil any values in this girl. As they walked she glanced again at the three cabinets, each containing a weapon: morning star, crossbow and musket. Something caught her eye in the last one. 'Look, it's Walter von Baugenwitz's gun.'

'Who?'

'You don't know the story?'

'Mum's the history freak, not me.'

'He was shot in a duel and died a long, agonising death.'

'Shit happens.'

Angela suddenly stopped and stared at the cabinet.

'What is it?' said Mike.

'The glass is on properly! Yesterday the lid was askew.'

'So?'

'Maybe somebody removed the musket and put it back in later.' Angela took a closer look at the weapon, the silver barrel, the decorative wooden butt, the polished rear sight.

Mike leaned over the cabinet too. 'It hasn't been used,' he said. 'There's no gunshot residue.'

This was confusing. No shot had been fired in the deaths of either Alexa or Philipp von Baugenwitz, yet Angela had a strong intuition that the musket was somehow connected to the murders.

They turned again into the smaller corridor that led to the steps to the dungeon. Angela's eyes fell on the chaise longue where Alexa von Baugenwitz had passed out in a drunken stupor on the night of the first murder. Thinking out aloud, she said, 'She wasn't drunk when she was with Wood.'

'She could certainly knock it back,' said Pia. 'But she only got really off her tits to annoy Philipp. Or sometimes she would just pretend to be wasted to embarrass him in front of other people.'

Not for the first time, Angela wondered if Alexa had only been acting drunk on the evening in question.

'You're overcomplicating this,' said Pia, opening the decorated wooden door to the steps.

175

'How so?'

'Do you know the principle of Occam's razor?'

'When there are several possible explanations for the same matter, choose the simplest,' said Angela. She wasn't surprised that the girl knew the principle too. Pia seemed to be at least as intelligent as her mother. The apple never falls far from the tree.

'Exactly,' said Pia, switching on the electric light rather than taking a torch from the wall, as her mother had on Angela's first visit. It seemed she didn't share Katharina's love of history. Why would she? In the continual present of a livestream existence, people on social media had no time for the past or future.

'So what do you think the simplest theory is?' asked Angela, as they descended the steps into the stuffy vault.

'Isn't it obvious? Philipp topped himself and Alexa followed suit.'

'But Alexa was going to tell me the name of Philipp's killer this morning.'

'What?' Pia sounded surprised. 'So she thought he was murdered too?'

'She did indeed.'

'Cool.'

'How is that cool?' said Mike. He was feeling increasingly vexed by this cocky teenager and her 40k a month.

'If it was a murder my clicks are going to go through the roof.'

'What did your parents do wrong?' Mike shook his head in disgust.

'Well to start with my mum killed my dad by driving

while she was shit-faced and wrapping the car around a tree,' Pia said, trying to sound as flippant as possible. But Angela detected the faint quaver in her voice. She thought how painful it must have been for her as a little girl, and no doubt still was today. How much energy it must cost her to mask the pain with cynical callousness...

And, she thought, it must be even harder for Katharina von Baugenwitz to live with the guilt of having killed her husband, the father of her daughter. No wonder she'd told Angela more than once that she'd do anything for Pia.

Angela felt even more sorry for the daughter than for her mother. The girl had a tragic background, just like Marie who as an orphan had lost her beloved Thea.

'I'm really sorry for what I said about your parents,' said Mike. He felt terrible. What did it matter how much the girl earned? No money in the world would be able to ease her suffering.

'No probs,' said Pia, back to her usual insouciant self. The three of them had now reached the door to the wine cellar that Mike had broken open yesterday. He wanted to go in first, but Angela held him back. 'Wait. I want to take a closer look at the wood.'

She examined the door all over and noticed something at the bottom. 'Do you see this, Mike? The wood here is cracked, like the door in the church when you tried to kick it open.

'And?'

'And the crack is big enough for a mouse to get through,' said Angela, delighted to have found a first piece of evidence.

'A mouse?'

'Yes – I saw one in the dungeon.'

Mike had no idea what Angela was getting at.

'The killer could be responsible for the broken bit at the bottom of this door.'

'But I broke it open yesterday.'

'You forced it open with your shoulder. Roughly at this level,' said Angela, pointing to a spot high up on the door. 'That wouldn't have caused a crack down there. Besides, although the door in the church is just as heavy as this one, the damage to it was much greater. Putin would have fitted through that crack.'

'What are you trying to say?' said Pia.

'That the person responsible for this crack must be weaker than Mike. Considerably weaker... maybe a woman.'

'Why would she have kicked it?' asked Pia. Angela mulled this over. The only logical explanation she could come up with was: 'Perhaps she was trying to force her way in because the door had been locked from the inside.'

'And why would she have wanted to do that?'

'Wait... I'm gradually getting an idea.' Angela's mind was working flat out, like the time she came up with the EU rescue packages that no one understood except for her and a handful of experts. Now she opened the door wide and carefully inspected the floor between the door and the table where she'd found the dead baron. 'Please don't come in yet,' she said to her companions.

'Why not?'

'The footprints.'

In the dust were hundreds of footprints, belonging to everyone who'd been at the crime scene: Angela, Mike, Inspector Hannemann, Lena, Katharina von Baugenwitz and the undertakers who'd removed the body in the knight's armour.

'The prints all merge into one another,' said Mike. 'You can't tell whose are whose.'

'But there are some that are so different that you can easily tell them apart. Here are Philipp's, for example.' Angela pointed to the print of an armoured boot. She carefully stepped onto the flags and reconstructed the path the baron had taken that night. 'He walked twice from the door to the table and once from the table to the door.' It was true: there were two prints right beside the door.

'So he paced up and down,' said Pia. 'What's your point?'

'I'll tell you in a moment, but first I have to make sure of one thing.' Angela motioned to the other two to join her in the cellar. 'Be careful not to efface the prints of the armoured boots.'

'Oh no!' Pia said with feigned horror. 'We might sabotage important detective work.'

Angela shot her a harsh look, the one she usually reserved for ministers who whispered in cabinet meetings. Unlike the ministers, who generally smiled sheepishly and then shut up, Pia kept talking. 'What's the point of all this anyway?'

'We're looking for further clues,' said Angela. The broken ink bottle still lay on the floor beside the table; the black ink had now dried on the stone.

'Looks like we've found one,' said Pia, pointing to prints that led further into the dungeon and weren't covered by any others.

'Those are women's shoes,' said Mike.

'You're lit,' remarked Pia.

'Thanks,' said Mike. It sounded like a compliment. Sort of.

Pia had the bit between her teeth now. 'Do you like wearing women's shoes?' she asked.

'What?'

'There's no need to feel ashamed. Many people, even macho bodyguards like your good self, have a fluid gender identity.'

'...'

'Sometimes you're this and sometimes you're that, right? Want some hashtags you can use for your Insta?'

'No, thank you! I really don't know what you're on about!'

'You can try #nonbinary, #genderfluid, #pansexual...'

Angela had stiffened. The mention of a hashtag had suddenly made her think of the 'α' again. But why? What did a hashtag have to do with it?

'Which woman made those prints?' said Mike, eager to move on from the insane idea that he might like wearing women's shoes.

'There's a very simple answer to that,' said Angela.

'Does that mean we know who the killer is?'

'Sadly not. Those are my footprints.'

'Of course!' Mike slapped his forehead.

'After we found the body I explored the length of the

cellar.' Angela glanced at the wine barrel, recalling how she'd thought the killer had hidden inside it. 'I was looking for a secret passage through which the killer could have escaped.'

Pia smiled patronisingly. 'This isn't Hogwarts, you know!'

'But there is a secret passage in the castle that goes from the boathouse to Alexa's bedroom.'

'Seriously?' Pia sounded genuinely surprised.

'Only it can't have anything to do with the killer's escape from the wine cellar.'

'Because it doesn't lead here,' said Pia.

'Precisely. No secret passage leads here, it seems.'

'What made you think there was a secret passage in the first place?'

'I saw a mouse running around. But it must have slipped in through the crack in the door. Also, there aren't any footprints except mine in this part of the cellar. If there had been a secret passage, the killer would have left traces—'

'Sounds plausible,' said Mike.

'… and that means she came through the door. But only once. She couldn't come in a second time – even though she wanted to.'

The baffled looks on her companions' faces were rather gratifying. For Angela was now convinced she had assembled enough pieces of the puzzle.

'Let us return to the table,' she said, trying her best not to sound triumphant, 'and I'll explain what happened here on the night of the murder.'

35

The three of them gathered around the table. Angela saw that the piece of paper with the 'ɑ' was no longer there. Why had Pia's talk of the hashtags reminded her of the letter? What was her subconscious trying to tell her?

'Right,' Mike said impatiently. 'How did it happen?'

'We're all ears,' said Pia.

'It was like this,' said Angela, dismissing the hashtags from her mind and sitting down. 'Right here at this table, Philipp and his killer had a conversation. The chalice of wine was in front of him. At some point she slipped the hemlock in his drink.'

'And he didn't notice?' said Pia.

'Not until he'd sipped it – from the bitter taste.'

'By which time it was too late,' said Mike.

'No… the pathologist told me that a mouthful wouldn't be enough. He would have needed to take three gulps.'

'So why did he keep drinking?'

'Because he was threatened with a weapon.'

'Seriously?' said Pia. 'Not the musket?'

'Yes, the musket. It explains why the glass lid to the cabinet wasn't on properly yesterday. The killer must have gone back to adjust it later.'

'But Philipp was in a full suit of armour,' said Mike. 'Why would he be worried about a musket?'

'The visor was open. Otherwise he wouldn't have been able to drink,' explained Angela.

'And a shot in the face at point blank range with a musket,' said Mike, shuddering, 'isn't a pleasant thought.'

'Like Walter von Baugenwitz in the duel. An agonising death, as you can see in the painting.'

'Better to drink the poison and get it over with quickly,' said Mike.

'Which is exactly what Philipp did.'

'I hate to be difficult,' said Pia, 'but that still doesn't explain the door locked from the inside.'

'After Philipp drank the poison,' said Angela, 'the killer left the room, certain that her work was done and that he would die at any moment. But, summoning the last reserves of his energy, Philipp struggled to his feet' – Angela struggled to her feet – 'then dragged himself to the door' – she dragged herself to the door – 'and locked it from the inside.' Angela pointed at the boot prints right beside the door.

'Why would he do that?'

'He wanted to write down the name of his killer and make sure she couldn't get rid of the evidence afterwards.'

'Ah,' said Mike.

'When the killer heard the key turn in the lock she guessed what he was going to do. She ran back but it was too late. In a panic, she shook the handle as hard as she could, wrenching it loose – that's why it fell off when you tried to get into the cellar, Mike.'

'I see,' said Mike.

'When she failed to force the handle, she kicked the door in fury. But that didn't help, of course. Or at least, it didn't help the killer.'

'Who did it help?'

'The mouse,' said Angela. She was enjoying herself.

'There's something I still don't get,' said Pia. 'Why didn't the killer use the musket to shoot the door open?'

'If she had, nobody would have believed it was a suicide.'

'In which case,' said Pia, 'shooting Philipp in the face was only ever an empty threat.'

'Philipp couldn't have known that.'

'But if the killer didn't break into the dungeon she ran the risk that Philipp would write her name and incriminate her.'

'Perhaps she heard the clank of the armour as Philipp collapsed onto the table. And the ink bottle smashing on the floor. She must have assumed that he hadn't managed to do it.'

'Assumed correctly.'

'Not quite.'

'He did do it?' said Pia. 'Then… you must know who killed him!'

'He only wrote a single letter of the name.'

Angela drew the 'a' in the dust with the tip of her shoe. 'Then he died.'

Pia looked at the letter.

'Do you know what it might stand for?' Angela asked.

'Alexa, obviously!' said Pia. 'And afterwards, overcome with guilt, she threw herself from the church tower. Like that other woman – what was her name again?'

'Adelheid von Baugenwitz.'

'That's the one. Just like my teacher always used to say – history repeats itself.'

'Actually your teacher was wrong. It never does, and it

didn't here. Inside the church we saw a figure dressed all in black. It was Alexa's murderer.'

'We think this person pushed Alexa from the tower,' explained Mike.

'Not quite,' Angela said. She was thoroughly enjoying the role of master-detective. 'She used the musket to force Alexa to go the top of the tower and then jump. Just as she had forced Philipp to drink the hemlock. Only this time when she put the musket back in the cabinet she replaced the glass lid correctly.'

'Two murders,' said Pia. 'This just gets better!'

'Don't you dare post all this on social media!' said Angela, realising what was on the girl's mind.

'Or you'll tell my followers that I'm a fake?' Pia seemed genuinely alarmed at this idea.

'That's precisely what I'll do.'

'I think I'll take the risk. The murder stuff is just too good.'

'You should see a psychologist,' said Mike.

'I've been through three already.'

'They're probably all in therapy themselves now,' said Mike.

'Let's do a deal, Pia,' Angela cut in. 'You can post everything once we've caught the murderer.'

Pia thought for a moment. 'Can I say I helped catch her too?'

'You're going to help our investigation?' said Angela disbelievingly.

'Duh, I'm not stupid enough to actually put myself in danger. I just want to post it.'

185

Angela thought hard. If she were to succeed in exposing the killer she wouldn't want it all over the papers. She'd never had a problem with other people taking the glory. Not that she was entirely lacking in vanity, but it was enough for her to know that she'd been the one pulling the strings behind the scenes. 'Agreed,' she said.

'Don't let me down,' said Pia.

'I love that,' said Mike. 'People who do bugger all but make plenty of demands.'

'I'm not doing "bugger all". Look, I'll give you a tip. Musket, hemlock, falling from the tower – it all adds up.'

'How so, exactly?'

'Whoever it was, she must be obsessed with the history of the von Baugenwitz family.'

'Like your mother, you mean?' said Angela.

'Are you mad?' said Pia, suddenly incensed. 'You know exactly who I mean!'

Angela did.

The only person without an alibi.

Marie, the tour guide.

Occam's razor.

When there are several possible explanations for the same matter, choose the simplest one.

36

Achim poured tea for everyone. Putin was dozing on a sunny patch of grass between some Hobbit garden gnomes and the wild roses that Angela loved so much. Everything had died on her balcony in Berlin because she was so seldom there, but here in this magical garden she couldn't get enough of the flowers being pollinated by bees and butterflies. Nurturing plants gave her almost as much pleasure as baking cakes, although this latest creation hadn't been anywhere near as fun as usual. She'd spent 94 per cent of the time dwelling on the fact that everything pointed to Marie being the killer. And the other 6 per cent feeling irritated that she hadn't been able to make a cherry tart because the only person selling fresh fruit in the village was that racist, the other Angela.

'Rmkbl,' said Mike, who had just shoved a colossal piece of cheesecake into his mouth.

Achim looked at him, an eyebrow raised quizzically.

Mike remembered that it was impolite to talk with your mouth full. He swallowed then said, 'Your wife is truly remarkable.'

The eyebrow rose a bit higher.

'No, no, I don't mean as a woman,' said Mike, embarrassed.

Angela wondered whether this comment was strictly necessary.

'I mean, she's not appealing in that way.'

That one certainly wasn't necessary.

'I'm just not into spring–late autumn relationships.'

'Mike! I think Achim has understood,' said Angela.

'Okay.' Mike shovelled in an even bigger piece of cheesecake. For the first time Angela realised that he didn't just eat for pleasure but to deal with stress too.

'To be honest, I still don't know what you're getting at,'

said Achim as he seated himself in a garden chair. 'I just wanted to know exactly what you find remarkable about my wife.'

'The way she worked out everything that happened in the wine cellar,' said Mike. 'It was sensational!'

Angela swelled with pride.

'I really have to apologise,' Mike told her. 'I totally underestimated you.'

'The story of my life,' said Angela, who loved being underestimated. She felt certain that it would play into her hands for the remainder of the investigation, just as it had in the early days of her political career.

'You're absolutely amazing!' added Mike.

None of her political colleagues had ever said that to Angela.

'Yes,' said Achim proudly. 'My wife really is remarkable. And very beautiful. The colour of her eyes, her cute little—'

'I think that's enough compliments for the time being,' said Angela. 'It's time to discuss the investigation.'

'Excellent idea,' said Mike. 'So – are we going to apprehend Marie?'

Angela knew it was high time to talk to Marie. But she didn't want Mike to accompany her. If Marie was indeed the killer it would need skill and subtlety to draw out a confession. 'I've got another job for you,' she told Mike. 'We have to exclude all other possible options.'

'Oh no, not that *Murder on the Orient Express* nonsense again.'

Angela chose to ignore this, even though that's

precisely what she had in mind. 'You're meeting Lena today, aren't you?' she said. 'I want you to go through all the alibis again. We have to rule out the possibility that Lena, Alexa and the other Angela worked together to wreak revenge on Philipp.'

'You mean I've got to question Lena?' Mike was clearly not pleased at the prospect.

'It's in your interest too.'

'How exactly?'

'Surely you don't want to go skinny dipping with a woman only to find out afterwards that she's a killer?'

'I don't want to go skinny dipping at all,' said Mike unhappily.

'You Westerners are such prudes,' said Achim.

Angela couldn't suppress a smile.

'Muffinella, how about we—'

'Not now, Achim. I've got a job for you too,' said Angela, sparing her bodyguard further discomfort.

'What do you want me to do?'

'You're going to interrogate the notary.'

'What for?'

'Maybe there *is* a secret heir amongst the suspects after all.'

'You really are clutching at every straw,' said Achim.

'At this point in the investigation we mustn't exclude anything,' said Angela quietly.

'Because you don't want Marie to end up in prison.'

'Yes,' said Angela, thinking of how Marie's baby might have to be put into state care. And if that happened, she would have to bear the blame.

Achim got up, wandered around the table and gave her a loving peck on the cheek.

'You're far too nice for this world,' said Mike.

Nobody in politics had ever said that to Angela either.

Life in this little town really was changing her.

37

Klein-Freudenstadt's deprived quarter had little in common with the problem areas in big cities. It consisted of two slightly run-down, thatched farmhouses that stood on the road out of the village, just before the place-name sign. The owner, who lived in Stuttgart, had converted them into six one-bedroom flats, each 40m² in size. The flats weren't in good condition; no repairs were ever carried out apart from those that were absolutely necessary.

As she stood outside holding a bunch of flowers from her garden, Angela looked at the building where Marie lived. A gutter had fallen off. Small mushrooms were growing on the thatch; that couldn't be good. The front garden was overgrown with all manner of weeds and wildflowers. She wondered whether there was hemlock among them – or perhaps behind the house?

Angela peered into the back garden but all she could see was a washing line, hung with everything from bedsheets to lingerie. Should she sneak in to have a proper search for the lethal plant?

No. Marie might be the chief suspect, but she'd come here to try to prove the young woman's innocence, not her guilt. She was well aware it wasn't going to be a pleasant evening. Even if Marie turned out not to be the killer, she was bound to be hurt when Angela confronted her with the suspicion. And she wouldn't want her helping with the birth anymore. The two would not become friends. Angela wouldn't be baking little Adrian any birthday cakes.

Perhaps she should just go? Achim and Mike would be furious if they found out that she'd put herself in harm's way again without protection: Angela had sworn she'd stay at home while Mike quizzed Lena and Achim sounded out the notary. Both men had checked to see if Angela was crossing her fingers behind her back – which she wasn't. But she *had* crossed her right big toe with its neighbour. Something she'd only done once in her life before, when in the midst of the financial crisis she'd promised the German people that their savings were secure.

Angela felt bad. Should she ring the bell or go home and prune the roses? She recalled a technique she'd often used in difficult situations: visualise a positive outcome rather than brooding over the potential negative consequences. Not that it had often helped. It hadn't helped her to negotiate a real peace for Ukraine with the Russian president, nor to elicit more than three sensible words from Trump at a time, nor to prevent Berlusconi from planting far too many soggy kisses on her cheek whenever they met. Still, at least it helped her go into meetings with a different mindset. So, to pep herself up, she envisaged the following scenario for the evening. It would transpire that the rumours were false: the dead baron wasn't the father of Marie's child after all. Which would mean she didn't have a motive for killing him and thus was innocent. As soon as that was sorted out the two women would enjoy a lovely *Star Wars* evening together – one that would herald the beginning of a wonderful friendship.

Angela overcame her hesitation and was about to ring the bell when she heard Marie call out from the window above. 'Just come in. The door's open. I live in the attic!'

There was such a warm smile on Marie's face that Angela regarded the positive outcome she'd just visualised as all but a *fait accompli*. She opened the door and cheerfully entered the building.

38

As he drove the electric car he loathed, Mike kept checking his mobile. Google Maps was meant to be taking him to the spot by the lake where he had arranged to meet Lena, but the mobile reception in the Uckermark was terrible. He was tempted to make a complaint to his new boss: how could she have so badly neglected the upgrading of the network during her time in office?

At last he reached what he hoped was the meeting point and climbed out of the cramped vehicle to look for Lena. Squinting into the sun, he spotted a figure standing on a jetty, but he couldn't make out who it was.

Mike quickened his step and made a beeline for the person he hoped was Lena.

As he neared the jetty, he still couldn't make out the face, but the sporty physique was unmistakable. The relief made him want to relax his pace, but his eagerness to see Lena again had the opposite effect. The net result of these two conflicting feelings was that he kept walking at the same speed. Lena greeted him with a beaming smile. She was wearing shorts and a T-shirt. Beside her was a picnic basket with a baguette, cheese and red wine. He was delighted. She must be counting on a lengthy evening! But after the cheesecake he could hardly allow himself any wine or baguette – and certainly not any cheese if he wanted to avoid humiliation on the scales tomorrow morning. How was he going to navigate these rocky shoals on a second date?

'There you are!' said Lena cheerfully, tearing Mike from his gloomy thoughts.

'Sorry... Google Maps...' he said.

'That won't work here until 2050 at the earliest!'

Mike smiled.

'How about we take a dip right away? I'm really hot!'

Mike was feeling warm under his suit too. But he knew it was nothing compared with how hot and bothered he'd get if he agreed. So he tried the same excuse he'd used yesterday: 'I haven't got any trunks.'

'You're so sweet,' said Lena.

When was the last time somebody had said that to him? He couldn't remember. But it certainly hadn't been after he'd uttered the words 'I haven't got any trunks'.

Without waiting for an answer Lena took off her T-shirt, catching Mike unawares. Even though he didn't want to stare, he couldn't help it. But his eyes didn't fix on what another man's might have – her breasts. Instead his gaze was caught by Lena's terribly scarred shoulder. It was no superficial graze; the baron had hit her full on with his shot. No wonder the injury had buried her Olympic dream. The old man was lucky he was already dead, thought Mike angrily.

Lena covered the shoulder with her hand. 'Men usually look elsewhere.'

'Sorry,' Mike said, bowing his head. He was embarrassed to look where men other men usually did.

'That's okay.'

Mike couldn't think what to say. He was desperate to make her feel better, but he didn't know how. Was it even possible to offer consolation for something like this?

'I'm jumping in,' said Lena, interrupting the silence. From the corner of his eye Mike could see that she'd slipped off her shorts too, but he immediately forced his gaze back down onto the boards of the jetty. He heard a splash. Only when Lena called out, 'What's up?' did he dare look in her direction. Her head was sticking out of the lake and her smile sparkled like the sun on the water. Once again Mike was tongue-tied; he was completely mesmerised by the sight of her.

'If you don't join me I'll have to go for a swim on my own,' she said, splashing about.

Mike was in a muddle. He wanted nothing more than to hold this woman in his arms, kiss her, protect her from all the injustice in the world, which included gunshot. But he felt ashamed.

'If you come in you'll get a kiss as a reward,' Lena said, swimming off.

'What the hell!' muttered Mike. He got undressed quicker than ever before in his life, took a run-up and dived headfirst into the lake.

39

The wallpaper had peeled off in many places, the stairs creaked and Angela wasn't keen on touching the hand-rail. Dinner smells mingled in the stairwell, everything from fried potatoes to curry. When she made it to the top floor Marie was standing at the door to her flat. She wore an apron emblazoned with the words: HOW THE MOTHER HALF LIVES. Probably a present from a friend in anticipation of the next eighteen years.

'Welcome to my little home!' said Marie. She seemed thrilled that Angela had actually come.

Angela handed her the flowers. 'They're beautiful!' said Marie, taking a sniff. Then she showed her guest into her flat, where Gloria Gaynor's 'I Will Survive' was play-ing. The tiny hall was pretty much filled by an IKEA coat rack and a houseplant, and through a half-open door Angela glimpsed a minuscule bathroom whose sickly green tiles may have been in vogue decades ago. Clearly 'flat' was a relative concept. The sitting–room–bedroom–kitchen contained a cooker and a few other units along with a bed, sofa bed, tatty armchair, wardrobe, table and baby-changing table. With perhaps three square metres of floor space in which you could stand. Assuming you weren't very tall, that is, for much of the room was under a sloping roof. She bet that hadn't been mentioned in the agent's description. It struck Angela that, although she'd made many policy decisions about benefits throughout her time at the helm of government, she hadn't once been inside the flat of a claimant. She'd been looking forward to leaving the Berlin bubble and meeting normal people. Now for the first time she felt it was actually happening.

'I'm making onion tart,' said Marie, moving to the kitchen area. 'The perfect supper for a film evening.'

Angela looked at the rolled-out dough, saw the ingredients, the onions and cubed bacon.

'Delicious! Can I help?'

'Oh, no, no. You're my guest!'

Angela could understand that. She never wanted guests to lend a hand when they came over. It was enough to have Achim by her side, even though he was anything but a help. Nosing around, she came across a faded photo pinned to a board: a picture of the castle from the 1980s. It was barely recognisable. The building was grey and unrenovated; before the fountain stood a cheerful bunch of children posing for a group photo. In the middle was Thea, the care worker and Marie's substitute mother, who'd taken her life. Thea's look of pride and fulfilment made it clear that the orphans had been her life's mission, while the children's laughing faces showed how happy they felt in her care. Far happier than the current inhabitants, thought Angela. The only black child in the group had a particularly big grin. Had she been teased by the other children at the orphanage because of the colour of her skin? With Thea in charge, Angela doubted it. What a woman she must have been!

Angela's gaze wandered to the baby-changing table. This might be her chance to bring up the question of the father and – assuming it wasn't Philipp von Baugenwitz – to relax and enjoy the rest of the evening.

'You've already got a changing table?' she asked.

'Yes, I made it myself,' said Marie, beaming proudly.

'Didn't the father help you?'

The smile vanished from Marie's face.

'Who is he, by the way?'

This was hardly the subtle approach Angela had had in mind.

'I don't want to talk about it.' Turning away, Marie took hold of a large, sharp knife to slice the onions.

'Is it Philipp?' Angela thought she'd better get it over with, even if she wasn't going to win 'Most Tactful Detective of the Year' award.

Marie glared at her. She was angry and full of pain.

'I'm sorry, but there are rumours in the village—'

Marie sliced with more energy.

'And you—' said Angela, feeling terrible before she'd even uttered the words, 'well, you knew the secret passage to Philipp's bedroom. And since the rug over the hatch wasn't dusty, I thought you might have used the passage—'

Marie was shaking with fury. 'I… DON'T… WANT… TO… TALK… ABOUT… IT!'

There were tears in her eyes that weren't from the onions. And she continued to slice with a rage that made Angela suddenly afraid of this woman wielding a knife.

197

40

Watson.

The penny had finally dropped. Achim *was* Watson rather than Sherlock Holmes. And the sooner he came to terms with it the better. Even in retirement the division of their roles would be the same as it had been throughout his whole time at this woman's side. Angela was Frodo Baggins, he was Samwise Gamgee. Angela was Captain Kirk, he wasn't even Spock, but Scotty. And now Angela was Sherlockella, while he was Watson.

Achim halted in the middle of the market square to consider whether this bothered him. After all, their life in Klein-Freudenstadt was supposed to be different from before. And indeed in many ways that was the case: he was spending more time than ever with his wife. What did it matter if he ended up merely being Dr Watson?

And what did 'merely' mean, anyway? Dr Watson had many fine qualities which Achim reckoned he shared: he was utterly loyal, had stamina and was a formidable opponent in combat. Okay, maybe the last one was stretching the comparison slightly, at least when it came to physical contests. But weren't backgammon, chess and his beloved Scrabble varieties of combat too? You bet they were! Only yesterday Achim had dealt his friend Tommy a lethal blow by laying PYXIDIUM on a 'triple word score'. Let someone else better that!

Achim might not be a Sherlock, but from now on he would be the best Watson who had ever existed outside of crime novels.

Fired by this self-proclaimed ambition, he made for a

café that stood right opposite the Hotel zum Dumpfsee, a pink half-timber building. He figured the notary must be staying there since it was the only hotel remaining in the village.

Achim Watson planned to find somewhere comfortable to sit outside and wait until the man entered the hotel. He'd order a rooibos caramel tea and peruse a textbook on fungal diseases, underlining words that could give him the edge in his next Scrabble contest. But no sooner had he sat down than Achim spotted a tall, gaunt man, around seventy and in a grey suit, heading for the hotel with his wheelie suitcase. It had to be the notary. The only other people who stayed at the Hotel zum Dumpfsee were terminally lost cyclists.

Dutifully casting aside all thought of refreshment, Achim stood up and hurried over.

'Hello!' he said as the man was heaving his suitcase up the entrance steps. 'My name is Achim Sauer. Sauer as in sweet, only the opposite.'

'My name,' replied the man in a sepulchral voice well suited to his profession, 'is Wolf Stark.'

'Corpses, worry not tho' 'tis dark, Your bequest is safe with Wolf Stark!' said Achim playfully.

'What?' The notary looked at Achim as if he had a screw loose. Clearly the man had no sense of humour, or at least none that overlapped with Achim's. Being a notary must be dull work indeed compared with the life of a quantum chemist. 'Please excuse me,' he said. 'I just thought it was a funny little rhyme.'

'You thought wrong.'

199

'So it seems,' Achim said trying to win the man over with a smile.

Rarely had one of his winning smiles been less victorious. Unfazed, he pressed on.

'You're the executor for the von Baugenwitz family, aren't you?'

'None of your business.'

'But you are, right?'

The gaunt man said nothing, his expression resembling that of an undertaker on duty.

'I'll take your silence as a "yes".'

'Who are you, anyway? A doctor?'

'What makes you say that?' Achim was confused.

'The book.' Stark gestured towards the volume on fungal infections.

'Ah… no, I'm just looking for words.'

'Words relating to fungal diseases?'

'Yes.'

'If you really aren't a doctor you must be a very strange fellow.'

'You wouldn't believe how often I've heard that.'

'Oh, I think I would.'

'I'm only reading the book to find good Scrabble words.'

At a stroke the notary's face brightened. 'You play too?'

'It's my passion.'

'Mine also.' The notary's thin lips formed into something that was almost a smile. 'I even play online.'

'So do I.'

'No!'

'Yes!'

'Perhaps we've played each other before.'

'What's your online handle?'

'Executor.'

Lawyers might have a way with words, thought Achim not for the first time, but their imagination was severely limited.

'Yours?'

'Lord Voldeboard. It's a Harry Potter reference.'

Stark looked blank. Clearly the man had never delved into anything so trivial and profane as popular literature.

'Well, since we haven't competed yet,' said Achim, 'what would you say to a game now?'

'A wonderful idea,' said Stark, an actual smile now playing around the corners of his narrow mouth. 'Please excuse me for being so dismissive just now.'

'That's alright,' Achim said. 'May I ask you a question?'

'I'll answer any question posed by a Scrabble friend.'

'Who's inheriting the von Baugenwitz family possessions?'

'Make that almost any question.'

'What if I let you in on a few incredible Scrabble words?'

'To do with fungal diseases?'

'From quantum chemistry. With them up your sleeve you'll win practically every game.'

'That certainly sounds enticing.' Stark pondered for a moment. 'How about you ask the questions and I'll see what I can answer with a good conscience.'

'Does Alexa von Baugenwitz have relatives who will now inherit the castle?'

'What I can tell you is that the castle never belonged to Alexa von Baugenwitz.'

'But surely Philipp left it to her? I mean, she was his wife.'

'The two of them had a marital contract. Alexa merely inherited a monthly widow's pension.'

Achim was flabbergasted. Neither he as Watson nor Angela as Sherlockella had considered this. The task he'd been assigned was to rule out the possibility that some hitherto unknown relative of Alexa might be in the frame as the killer. But now there was a completely different question to answer: 'So who is inheriting everything from Philipp?'

'I can't name names.'

'But surely,' said Achim, trying to channel his wife's powers of persuasion by building a bridge for the notary, 'you can say, in very general terms of course, what relationship someone must have with the deceased in order to inherit.'

'I can.'

'And?'

'In a case such as this one, the child inherits.'

'But Philipp von Baugenwitz didn't have any children.'

'I can't name names.'

Achim racked his brains. All that came to mind was the rumour that Marie was carrying the baron's baby. And even if this was true, the child was illegitimate. Surely it couldn't inherit.

Or could it?'

'I've got another general question.'

'Fire away.'

'Can an illegitimate child inherit?'

'It never ceases to amaze me,' observed Stark, 'how shrewd Scrabble players are.'

41

Marie lay the knife on the chopping board and held her tummy. She was so distraught that it appeared to be having an effect on the baby. For a moment Angela was worried that the contractions would start. Although she'd promised to accompany Marie to the hospital and even to the labour ward, it was one thing to talk the talk, quite another to actually walk the walk. Angela was reminded of the refugee crisis when, before the country's assembled media, she'd said, 'We can do this.' It would have been wiser to put it in a more open-ended way, for example: 'Wouldn't it be great if we could do this?' Or else: 'It would be ridiculous, wouldn't it, if we couldn't do this?' Or best of all: 'Ladies and Gentlemen, I've said what I have to say. Outside there is coffee and cake waiting for you.'

'Is everything alright?' asked Angela.

'Yes,' said Marie, looking far from alright. She took several deep breaths, then wiped the sweat from her brow with the sleeve of her blouse. As she rolled it up, she revealed a scar on her wrist. Angela swallowed; the poor woman had actually tried to take her own life.

Marie noticed that Angela was staring at the scar. The two of them said nothing for a while. 'It's not that old, is it?' said Angela at last.

203

Marie said nothing.

No answer was still an answer.

Angela was reluctant to ask more questions, but she must if – as she very much hoped – she was going to prove Marie's innocence. 'Did you do it because Philipp left you?'

Again, no answer was an answer.

'But before you knew you were pregnant by him?'

'I'd never do anything to hurt my child!' Marie's eyes flashed angrily.

'And I never would have thought you would,' said Angela, raising her hands defensively.

'Good!'

'Philipp's death has affected you deeply, hasn't it?' said Angela, trying to make progress.

Now Marie wasn't just cross, she was sad too. Did she still have feelings for the man? Or was she just bitter about the fact that her boy would never have the opportunity to know his father?

'But not Alexa's death today, it seems?'

'She hated me after she heard about the baby! She abused me, threatened to scratch my eyes out! She was trying to force us out of Klein-Freudenstadt. Why would I shed any tears for her?'

Angela realised this outburst was confirmation that the baby in Marie's tummy was the baron's. 'I believe the two of them were murdered,' she said.

'What…?!' Marie sounded shocked. But was that because she'd had no idea about the murders, or because she herself was the murderer and was now being confronted with her crime? Or just acting? Right now the second and third of these no longer seemed quite so absurd.

Angela glimpsed one last chance to prove Marie's innocence. She recalled the immortal words of the goal-keeper Oliver Kahn, picturing him during her visit to the German national team changing room when he'd been clad in nothing but a skimpy towel: 'Keep going, just keep going!'

'Our assumption,' she said calmly, 'is that the murders were carried out by someone with an excellent knowledge of Klein-Freudenstadt's history.'

'You think that I…?!'

'No, I don't!'

'Well, thank you!' said Marie.

'Still, it can't be denied that you have a motive. Philipp abandoned you with a child whose paternity he refused to acknowledge. And Alexa wanted to drive you and your baby from the village.'

Marie placed her hands over her tummy as her eyes filled with tears of despair and anger.

'Not only that, Philipp's family claimed back your childhood home. The orphanage had to be closed. And your beloved Thea…' Angela looked at the photo. 'She never got over it and took her own life.'

Marie steadied herself with a hand on the work surface, not far from the chopping board with the knife.

What would Angela do if she attacked her?

Now she was hoping for her own sake as well as Marie's and the baby's that the woman was innocent.

But after outlining all the potential motives, she was no longer so sure.

Keep going, just keep going!

'There's even a clue left by the dead man that points at you.'

'What clue?'

'May I, for the purposes of demonstration?' Angela went over to the chopped onions. Her plan was not just to shape them into an 'a', but to place herself between Marie and the knife.

'By all means,' said Marie, removing the knife from the board. It was possible that she just didn't want her guest to cut herself by accident. But Angela wasn't so sure.

Keep going...

As she remembered Oliver Kahn's words and Achim's reaction to them, Angela couldn't help grin. 'Can't you stay out of the changing rooms of these fit, half-naked footballers?' he had grumbled. It was astonishing what came to mind when you were in danger...

'Why are you grinning like that?' asked Marie.

... just keep going...

Angela shaped the onions on the board into an 'a'.

'What's that supposed to be?'

'It's what Philipp scrawled before he died.'

'Onions?'

'No, no! The "a" – it's the clue I was talking about.'

'But what's it got to do with me?'

'It's the first letter of your son's name. Adrian.'

Marie stared at Angela and began to laugh out loud. She was still clutching the knife.

42

'What's so funny?' asked Angela. She looked around furtively for an escape route. It wasn't far to the door. And in her state Marie was not particularly mobile. But Angela wasn't athletic. If only she'd taken Emmanuel Macron's advice and hired a fitness trainer!

'That "a" is what's funny,' panted Marie, pointing at the onions.

'I don't understand,' said Angela.

'How could you?' To Angela's relief Marie put the knife to one side.

'If Philipp had wanted to give a clue about our child he would have written this.'

Marie arranged the onions into a 'B'.

'Sorry. I still don't understand.'

'When he found out about the baby,' explained Marie, 'he insisted that I name him Benedikt.'

'But he refused to recognise the child!'

'He still thought he had the right to choose the name. That's how he was.'

'But you wouldn't agree?'

'Of course not. But I never told him I was going to call the baby Adrian.'

So the 'a' wasn't a clue to the child's name. Assuming Marie was telling the truth.

'Look,' said Marie, picking up her mobile and showing Angela a text message from Philipp on the day he died.

I've changed my mind. I won't acknowledge little Benedikt publicly, but

I'll transfer you 1,000 Euros every month for him. :-)

So it seemed Marie was telling the truth. The baron, though clearly a master of the inappropriate smiley, had not known that his son would go by the name Adrian.

'Did you refuse the money?'

'I accepted it for the sake of the little one.' Marie showed Angela the next text message where she'd given him her account number. 'But there won't be anything now that he's dead.'

As she looked at the '**B**' that wasn't an '**a**', Angela felt a surge of relief. Not just because she was no longer in danger, but because it meant Marie was innocent.

'Do you still think I might be a killer?'

Angela began to feel ashamed. Part of her really had suspected her friend. 'I'm really very sorry.'

'It's alright,' said Marie.

'I ought to go now.' Angela reckoned she had forfeited the right to enjoy Marie's hospitality.

'Are you deaf? I said it's alright.'

'But I've meddled in your private affairs.'

'Yes, even worse than the case manager at the job centre!'

'And I offended you with my suspicions.'

'You can say that again.'

'So how can it be alright.'

Marie went over to the pinboard and tapped the photograph with her finger. 'Do you know what Thea always said?'

'What?'

208

'You always have to give people a second chance.'

'And that's what you're doing now?'

'It's how I was brought up.'

Angela was touched. She looked more closely at Thea in the photo, standing amongst the children and smiling. Perhaps it would have been more inspiring for the people if someone like Thea had made her way to the chancellery instead of me, she thought.

'Nobody's perfect,' said Marie.

'Very true,' said Angela replied. The two women were both smiling.

'What now? Onion tart and *Star Wars*?'

'Yes! Onion tart and *Star Wars*!' Angela felt liberated as never before.

43

Achim stirred the milk into his rooibos caramel tea and thought about his wife. It would make Angela sad to hear that Marie had another motive for murder, assuming that Philipp really was the father of her child. Angela had taken the girl into her heart. And it was a big heart. Yes, Angela was a tender, sensitive woman. Even if Achim was the only person in the whole wide world who knew this. Including Angela herself. She believed she'd been hardened by all those years in politics. But Achim knew this wasn't the case. The opposite, in fact – his Muffinella had become more vulnerable because she'd had to hide her feelings and keep them in check for so long. Like a dam behind which too much water accumulates and which collapses with the tiniest crack, flooding the entire Netherlands. And Belgium. And parts of North-Rhine Westphalia. As far as Hamm.

Achim suspected that if Marie really was the killer then Angela would weep for the first time this millennium. And go on weeping for a long time. But... maybe it would do her good to allow her tears to flow?

'If you keep stirring like that the milk's going to turn into cheese,' said the notary, who'd already drunk half his own rooibos caramel tea.

Achim stopped stirring.

'Do you know what?' he continued. 'You haven't asked all the important questions yet. Not by a long shot.'

'What other questions should I be asking?'

'That's for you to work out.' Stark cut in half the iced doughnut he'd bought from a bakery. A few moments earlier the waiter had pointed out that you weren't allowed to eat your own food at the café, but Stark had easily countered this with various paragraphs of the law, their sub-paragraphs and sections, as well as a landmark judgment by Erlangen district court. 'Okay, okay, eat it!' the defeated waiter had said. 'Just don't tell my boss.'

As he gazed at the dissected doughnut, oozing with jam, Achim mulled over what question he should ask. A Sherlock would know, as would a Sherlockella, no doubt. But even a Watson was a good investigator. Better than Inspector Lestrade, at any rate. And so he, the best Watson outside the pages of crime fiction, should be able to do the same!

Achim fuelled his brain cells with a sip of tea. He'd

found out that the unborn child would inherit money. Which his mother would manage. So it was practically hers. That much was clear. Stark wouldn't say how much money it was. But perhaps...

'Does an illegitimate child inherit everything?'

'Depends.'

'On what?'

'On whether it's the only child.'

'But Philipp doesn't have any other children.'

Stark grinned and forked an eighth of the doughnut into his mouth.

'Does he?'

'This doughnut is absolutely sensational! Wurst is the best baker for miles around,' said Stark.

'Don't let my wife hear you say that.'

'Next time I'll get not one but two doughnuts,' said Stark, winking.

'Have you got something in your eye?' said Achim.

'You're not very good at subtle clues, are you?'

'What was the subtle clue?'

'Not one but *two* doughnuts.'

'How is doughnuts a clue?'

'Two!'

'Two?'

'Most people would say "Bingo!" at this point. But I prefer "Scrabble!"'

'Philipp von Baugenwitz has two children?' Achim could barely believe it.

'You said it, not me,' said Stark, savouring another eighth of the doughnut.

211

44

Since Mike had begun his job in the Uckermark several things had occurred that he hadn't expected. For example that he'd investigate a murder case, that he'd consume industrial quantities of BMI-raising cake, or that he'd constantly be clearing up Putin's mess. But most astonishing of all was that he was now swimming naked in a lake with a gorgeous younger woman, who was also naked.

'You see,' said Lena, giggling, 'it's not so hard is it?'

Her laughter was so enchanting that Mike forgot his shame. 'No, it's not!' he laughed.

And in truth, nothing in his life had ever felt as easy as this.

'Come closer,' said Lena seductively.

'Erm, do you mean...?' Mike was treading water about half a metre away.

'I promised you a kiss. And my neck's not that long.'

Now it no longer felt easy, but exciting.

'You're blushing!'

'No, no, it's just when I'm in the water the blood rushes to my head.'

'You're so sweet.' Lena swam up to Mike, took his large head in her hands and kissed him. It was a wonderful kiss, the perfect mixture of passion and tenderness. He'd experienced passion with his ex-wife, but no tenderness. More like flying plates. Smashed vases. Hurled toilet brushes.

'Why are you grimacing?'

'I was just thinking of my ex-wife.' Mike's inability

to lie had got him into trouble more than once in his life.

'That's not very nice,' said Lena, pulling away.

'I was comparing your kisses to hers.'

'Neither is that!'

'Hers were never as nice as yours.'

'Lena was bemused. 'Okay... that's a bit better I guess.'

Mike looked at her. Why did he always sour these lovely moments? He was such an idiot! A champion idiot! If there was a world cup for idiots no one else would even bother competing because they'd know they didn't stand a chance. Even Kanye West would stay at home.

'Shall we have our picnic?' said Lena.

Mike guessed this wasn't the time to bring up the effects of cheese and wine on his BMI. So he merely nodded. His eyes alighted on Lena's shoulder again, the drops of water glistening on the scars in the evening sun. 'Does it still hurt?'

'Yes.'

Mike wished he could take away this lovely woman's pain.

'Why are you staring at me like that?' Lena suddenly looked uncertain.

Mike didn't reply.

'What are you thinking about?'

'I'd love to be able to take away your pain,' he said, once more unable to lie.

'Well, I've got the money for the operation in Fort Lauderdale. I'm having it done in two months.' Somehow she didn't sound very happy about it.

'It's a hell of a lot of money though.' Mike was thinking how unfair it was that she had to pay so much to fix something that wasn't her fault.

'Yes… it is,' said Lena, still sounding strangely uncertain. Mike even thought she came across as kind of… *guilty*?

'Is anything wrong?' asked Lena.

'No, no,' said Mike, not sounding particularly convincing. He wondered where the money had come from. Police officers usually found it almost impossible to put money aside. And an operation in the United States wasn't something any bank would give a loan for. Should he quiz Lena on this?

Evidently the expression on Mike's face spoke volumes, because before he could decide Lena had seen what was on his mind. 'None of this is any of your business!' she snapped.

She turned and swam towards the jetty. Mike didn't follow her, just trod water sadly. He realised he had begun to mistrust Lena. In a very different way from his ex, who he'd never believed when she claimed to be out with her best friend until four in the morning and only smelled of aftershave because she'd hugged her friend's husband. He mistrusted Lena in a no-normal-police-officer-suddenly-has-25,000-euros-up-their-sleeve sort of way.

45

Angela was amazed that an evening which had started so badly could have gone so swimmingly. The onion tart had been delicious – better than many a three-star menu at state receptions. Indeed, incomparably excellent compared to the snails in gorgonzola that she had once been served at a dinner with François Hollande. The wine, which of course Angela had drunk on her own, had also been surprisingly good. Even the *Star Wars* film had defied her expectations. Okay, you couldn't get too profound when thinking about the plot. Strictly speaking, Luke Skywalker had committed a war crime. In destroying the Death Star he'd risked a vast amount of collateral damage, because it wasn't just Imperial troops on the Death Star but civilians, for example cleaning staff. And Angela had enjoyed the flirting between Princess Leia and Luke only until Marie revealed that they were in fact brother and sister. From then on she kept her fingers crossed for Han Solo; the man had a certain wicked charm. A bit like George W. Bush, only far more intelligent.

She and Marie were now outside. The moon, almost full, shone as it wouldn't in Berlin again until electric cars were the norm and heavy industry signed up to standards that Greta Thunberg could only dream of.

'I'll walk you home,' said Marie.

'Oh, don't worry,' said Angela. 'I moved to Klein-Freudenstadt especially so I'd be able to wander on my own from time to time.'

'Okay. But you're the one who thinks there's a murderer on the loose, not me!'

Angela wished Marie hadn't reminded her. This *Star Wars*–onion tart evening was the first time since finding the body in the wine cellar that she hadn't thought of the murder investigation. Was she putting herself in danger by going home alone? After all, she was the only person who was a threat to the killer. But was her sleuthing really being taken so seriously that somebody would run the risk of attacking her? It seemed unlikely. The killer, whoever she might be, was hardly being backed into a corner. Besides, it would be wrong for Marie to accompany her – exposing a pregnant woman to that sort of threat would be downright irresponsible.

'No killer's going to be that stupid,' said Angela, crossing her fingers.

'Up to you,' said Marie. 'But we absolutely have to have another film evening.'

'I'd love to.' Angela was delighted at the offer. It meant that Marie had enjoyed the evening. And that meant Angela was in the process of finding a friend in her new home!

'Let's watch *Eat Pray Love!* next time,' beamed Marie.

'All three sound good to me.'

'Can I have a hug?'

Angela was momentarily astonished. But then she felt pleased and said, 'Of course!' Marie embraced her warmly. It was a lovely feeling. And it was followed by a different, no less lovely, but unusual and even slightly uncanny one: the baby kicked against Marie's tummy and thus against Angela's as well. Once. Twice. Three times.

'Adrian likes you too!' laughed Marie.

Angela turned red. With joy. Was it possible to have grandmotherly feelings if you weren't a grandmother?

Marie freed herself from the embrace. 'I'm so thrilled you're going to be there at the birth.'

If Angela had been taken off-guard when she'd first been asked, now, after their evening and the three kicks to her stomach, she felt better prepared. She was really looking forward to supporting Marie in this important moment of her life. 'I'm thrilled too.'

'Then I'll say goodnight!'

'Goodnight!'

The two women smiled at each other, then Angela set off for home. After a few steps she heard the door close behind her. Marie had gone back inside. In a jaunty mood, Angela strolled down the road that was lit by the moon, stars and the odd streetlamp. Past gardens, graves, trees and a few scattered houses, their inhabitants already asleep. Angela breathed in the springtime evening air and felt again the little kicks that Adrian had given her.

The miracle of life.

Who'd have thought that she'd come into contact with it again?

This little corner of the world was full of surprises.

And Angela didn't have to wait long for the next one.

For an arrow hissed past, missing her by a whisker, and slammed into a tree behind.

46

Run! cried all Angela's instincts, but all she could do was stare at the arrow, still quivering in the trunk of the tree.

Run! her instincts cried again, louder this time. Yet she remained rooted to the spot.

What the hell are you waiting for, you stupid cow! her instincts yelled. And although Angela knew that her instincts were correct, she thought their tone was slightly off. Before she could raise this point, however, the second arrow sped past so close that her hair ruffled in its draught. This one thudded into the tree trunk too.

Angela knew she had to heed the advice of her instincts. Even though running wasn't her forte. When was the last time she'd sprinted? Probably on the day the Wall came down, when she heard Achim shout, 'Quick, quick, you'll never guess what old Schabowski has just said! Everyone's allowed into the West!' She'd been in the sauna at the time, but she'd covered the ground from there to the nearest television faster than Katrin Krabbe. And this without even taking clenbuterol. Now she was being hunted like a wild animal but couldn't seem to budge.

RUUUUUUN!

Angela wished there was some other activity she could undertake to save her life. Why couldn't her instincts shout, 'Manage a crisis meeting,' or 'Explain string theory,' or 'Set out the COVID regulations for the thousandth time'? But no, it had to be 'Run!'

Finally she was freed from her paralysis and got moving. Just in time, for the third arrow went whistling past her back to join its siblings in the tree.

Angela ran faster than she ever had before, not excepting that time in 1989. Still, she couldn't help thinking of the Donald Duck cartoons that Achim loved to watch on YouTube.

STOP THINKING SUCH NONSENSE AND FOCUS ON RUNNING!

Angela now realised why she always had such absurd thoughts in dangerous situations – they took her mind off the terror.

Another arrow landed right by her feet, on a strip of green between her and the ditch.

RUN BACK THE OTHER WAY! her instincts squealed in panic. Panting, Angela stared at the arrow. It dawned on her that her instincts weren't particularly helpful. Run as she might, sooner or later she'd be hit, and the way she was already gasping for breath it was likely to be sooner.

Searching frantically for a way out, Angela saw a ditch. A plan formed in her mind: if she leapt into it she couldn't be hit, for a while at least. And she could use this precious time to make an emergency call with her mobile. Without further ado, therefore, Angela leapt into the ditch.

Like so many plans forged under severe time pressure, this one also manifested weaknesses during its execution. Angela hadn't, for example, calculated how deep the ditch was. As a result she found herself standing in cold water up to the second button on her blazer. She hastily reached inside her pocket, but it was too late. Her mobile was wet and thus unusable. Here was one disadvantage of swapping your ultra-modern, water-resistant work phone for an old Nokia brick.

What could she do? Should she climb out the other side of the ditch and keep running? That option would, she estimated, give her a 0.5 per cent chance of survival. The only alternative she could come up with in her panic was to submerge herself and hope that the archer wouldn't find her in the dirty water.

No sooner had she squatted under the water than it occurred to her she ought to have found a reed or bit of straw to breathe through. Should she surface again? No, it was too dangerous.

Angela wondered how long she would be able to hold her breath. Fifty seconds? Maybe sixty at a push. Was this how she was to spend the final minute of her life – in a ditch full of brackish water and goodness only knew what other unsavoury matter?

Had she not been underwater Angela would have chuckled at the irony. All those years as a politician, more than fifteen as chancellor, and never once had her life been in danger, despite the many enemies she had at home and abroad. It was only after moving to sleepy Klein-Freudenstadt that she'd fallen victim to an assassin.

But if she had to die, then let it be with a modicum of dignity. Not gasping for air because she'd remained underwater until the last moment, but looking the killer – whoever that might be – squarely in the eye. That way at least she would have solved the case before she sank to the ground, an arrow in her chest.

So Angela didn't wait until she was out of air, but surfaced after thirty seconds. Dripping, her wet hair sticking to her face.

She stood like that for while, but couldn't see anybody. Nor did any more arrows fizz her way, though she did see the lights of a car approaching. And footsteps running off. It seemed that the killer had fled.

Angela almost whooped and threw her arms in the air like she had at the Macaraña Stadium in Rio de Janeiro when Mario Götze scored to win the World Cup. But now the car came to a hard stop right by the ditch. Had the killer called for back-up? The *Murder on the Orient Express* theory was, after all, still the most plausible one on offer.

The car door opened and footsteps approached the ditch.

Angela's heart was pounding wildly. She prepared herself to look fate in the eye.

A torch shone in her face. She couldn't make out who was holding it, but the voice that now spoke was very familiar.

'I don't think I want to know what you're doing down there.'

'No,' Angela replied, hugely relieved. 'No, you don't, Mike.'

47

In silence the two of them got out of the car outside the half-timber house where Angela lived. Mike had wrapped a blanket around his boss after pulling her out of the ditch, but hadn't said a word after explaining that he'd found her by locating her mobile – which he'd felt compelled to do because yet again she'd sneaked out on the sly.

'We're not going to tell Achim my life was in danger,' whispered Angela at the front door.

Mike just nodded. His silence was not reproachful, it came from real concern for her life. Angela could understand why. The assassination attempt had turned her detective game into something deadly serious. But something else seemed to be oppressing him. Had something happened during his evening with Lena?

Despite the fact that she was technically freezing, Angela suddenly felt hot all over. Of course! Who else would use a bow and arrow as a weapon? How silly not to think of it before! Still, when you were running for your life, sober analysis wasn't easy.

Angela looked at Mike. Should she talk to him about Lena now? Before she could wonder any further, Achim opened the door.

'Goodness gracious!' he exclaimed. 'What on earth happened to you?'

Angela had never been able to lie to her husband. Maybe the odd minor twisting of the truth, that had never been a problem. But when it was a really important matter, she found it impossible to deceive this wonderful man. And yet he mustn't know the truth! The worry would make him sick.

She looked pleadingly at Mike. As Angela was only too aware, her bodyguard was not in the habit of lying for his bosses, no matter how much they begged him to. But for Angela he now cast his principles aside.

'I was trying to locate your wife, but because these stupid electric cars don't make a sound she didn't see me until it was too late and she leapt into a ditch in fright,' he said.

'Oh you poor thing!' Achim took his wife in his arms and hugged her tightly. He didn't care that she was still wet. Angela gave Mike a furtive look of gratitude. He nodded back curtly, as if to say, 'You're welcome.' Angela realised how fond they'd all become of each other.

Achim led Angela to the bathroom where she removed her wet clothes and took a hot shower. Then she put on the things her husband had got out for her: her favourite purple silk pyjamas and the white towelling dressing gown she'd picked up from a hotel in the Tyrol twenty years ago. Although it was quite frayed now it was so cosy she'd couldn't bear the thought of replacing it.

Thus swaddled, Angela entered the kitchen, where Mike was at the table drinking a cup of tea. He was evidently deep in thought; Angela could practically see the dark clouds circling above his head. When she sat down Putin cantered over and snuggled up against her dressing gown. Achim poured her a cup of rooibos caramel tea. As soon as she'd taken a sip, Mike said, 'We've got to stop this.'

'Stop what?' asked Achim, whereas Angela of course knew what he was getting at.

'The investigation needs to be taken over by professionals.'

'Do you mean Inspector Hannemann?' said Achim.

'Professionals, I said.'

'Lena?'

The dark clouds above Mike's head thickened.

'We can't give up,' Achim went on. 'We're so close to the solution. I talked to the notary earlier. Alexa von Baugenwitz never inherited the castle and estate from Philipp – the two of them had a pre-nuptial agreement.'

'So who is inheriting?' said Angela, surprised.

'Marie's illegitimate child.'

Now Angela was more than surprised. She was gobsmacked. Almost dumbfounded. This gave her pregnant friend – yes, she was her friend! – another motive. Philipp's text message meant she could prove the baron was the father and register a claim on the inheritance. And yet she felt able to reply with utter conviction, 'Marie is innocent.'

'Has she got an alibi?' asked Achim.

'No.'

'So how do you know she's innocent?'

'My heart tells me.'

'Not just your intuition?'

'No.'

'Then she really must be innocent.'

'Do you actually believe me?' Angela was touched.

'There's only one thing in this world I trust more than your intellect. And that's your heart.'

Angela couldn't help but smile.

'And that means,' Achim went on, 'we need to turn our attention to the other heir.'

'The other heir?'

'Philipp had another child.'

'Who is it?!' Angela could scarcely contain herself. She felt far more tense than while waiting for the Bundestag election results, when the only question was whether she'd end up leading a black-red or a black-yellow coalition.

'Sadly the notary refused to reveal their identity,' said Achim.

'Could it be Lena?'

'The age would be about right.'

'Didn't I just say we should leave this investigation to the professionals?' growled Mike. 'This is a case for the Federal Police!'

'But these are local crimes,' said Achim. 'The Federal Police would only show up if someone was trying to kill Angela, which thank God isn't the case.'

At this Mike looked away shiftily, as did Angela. She began awkwardly stroking Putin with one hand, while holding her tea in the other.

Achim was confused.

'I said,' he repeated, in an attempt to get to the bottom of the matter, 'thank God that isn't the case.'

'I think Putin needs to go to beddy-byes,' said Angela.

'Angela?'

'He needs his sleep.'

'Were you attacked?'

'I'll take him to his basket.'

'Good God!'

Angela saw the panic in her husband's eyes. And now she was worried. Not about herself, but for Achim. How would he get by on his own if she were killed? It had always been obvious to her that she had to outlive him.

Yes, losing him would be unbearable, but he would simply fall apart if she went first.

The thought made her drop her cup, which smashed on the tiles. Putin lapped up the tea. But this passed Angela by – all she wanted to do was to dispel her husband's fear.

'Mike, you're right,' she said. 'We're going to stop playing detectives and I'll call the Federal Police Bureau.'

48

Angela was one of only about twenty people in Germany who had the contact details of the Bureau chief: his mobile number, which he always answered at once; and his email address, from which he always wrote back promptly. No matter what time of day or night.

At first Angela wanted to ring, but then she thought it would be more effective to consolidate all the findings from the investigation in writing. So she sat in her white dressing gown at the antique desk in her small study. It was stuffed with books she'd never been able to read during her political career, including biographies of Shakespeare, novels by Elena Ferrante and an antiquarian edition of the collected works of Jane Austen.

In her email Angela described the deaths, listing all the people who could be considered suspects: Katharina von Baugenwitz, her daughter Pia, the farmer Angela Kessler, the policewoman Lena Amadeus, and – despite what her heart said – Marie. She also set out the individual alibis, mentioning that Katharina, Lena and the other

226

Angela could vouch for each other. Pia had no alibi for Alexa von Baugenwitz's murder, while Marie didn't have one for either killing. Put like that, things didn't look good for Marie, but Angela felt certain that the Bureau would prove her innocence.

Angela didn't omit the attempt on her own life. She'd even asked Mike to return to the scene to secure the arrows and take photographs of them. They had noticed that the arrows were too small for a normal bow – though they would certainly fit the crossbow in the glass cabinet next to the one with the musket. Did this suggest Lena wasn't the killer? Or the opposite: that she was coming and going in the castle as if the place already belonged to her?

Angela decided to put these theories out of her mind. It was now a case for the Federal Police. Her amateur sleuthing was at an end!

When she'd finished, Angela read back through her email, as she always did when it was something important. She was convinced that the world's angst levels would fall by 50 per cent if it was forbidden to send the first draft of an email, text, or WhatsApp message.

As she read it through from the beginning for the second time – twice checked was twice as good – she noticed something. Suddenly she understood why she'd been so fixated on the hashtags while they were in the wine cellar. Why the character had reminded her of the baron's final note. Now she knew what he had been trying to say.

Not just that, Angela knew who the killer was.

Pushing her chair back from the desk, she took a

deep breath and reviewed all her findings once again in the light of this breakthrough. Then she decided against sending the email to the Bureau chief. She would solve this case herself after all!

She just had to check some open access information about what happened when someone died without a will and scrutinise one of the four alibis a little more carefully. Then she would be ready to round up all of the suspects for a slice of cake tomorrow afternoon and make her grand reveal.

<h1 style="text-align:center">49</h1>

'Shit, that is good!' said the other Angela as she tasted ex-chancellor Angela's chocolate cake. Despite her feelings about her namesake, the latter couldn't help being pleased. The two of them were sitting at a large table in Angela's magical garden, together with the rest of the suspects. Achim served tea and coffee, while Mike stood to one side, observing the proceedings. Putin squatted beside Katharina von Baugenwitz, hoping for a morsel or two.

None of the other suspects had touched their cake. Pia was the only one who drank some coffee. Other than that she was as taciturn as the others. Her single comment so far had been about Achim's Hobbit garden gnomes, which she'd posted on Instagram with the caption 'Extinction Level Event', whatever that meant.

All the women looked ill at ease. They were only here because Mike had invited each of them in turn, saying that the meeting was about new information relating to the baron's bequest. Marie was the only one who'd accepted Angela's invitation just because she wanted to see her friend.

Now Angela tapped a cake fork against a water glass. Everyone turned to her.

'Welcome to my new home!'

No response. No smiles. Apart from Marie.

'Or, I should say, our new home,' Angela added, looking towards Achim.

'I've invited you all here to talk about the murders of Philipp and Alexa von Baugenwitz.'

At this point Angela had expected some protest that these were suicides rather than murders. But there was total silence. Katharina, Lena and the other Angela stared at the table. Pia slipped her mobile into the large shoulder bag that she'd put beside her chair. Even Marie stopped smiling. Clearly the women around the table had accepted that Inspector Hannemann's theories were wrong.

'First I would like to explain how the murders were carried out. Then we will examine who might benefit from the deaths and is, therefore, a suspect.'

'I thought you were going to give us new information about the inheritance,' said the other Angela.

'And I will do so – but that information is closely connected to the murders.'

'I'm only interested in what will happen to my lease.'

'I'm not sure that's quite true,' said Angela.

'What is this? I'm automatically a suspect because I happen to be in the "wrong" party?'

'Just as you automatically suspected Marie because of the colour of her skin?' said Angela.

Marie flinched at this. Angela mentally chided herself – she mustn't let herself get carried away. She wanted to give her friend a smile, but saw that Marie was clutching her stomach in discomfort. With all the excitement little Adrian must be kicking harder than ever.

'Are you going to enlighten us?' said Pia.

'All in good time.' Angela began to describe the 'how' of the first murder. How the baron noticed that hemlock had been put into his wine. How the killer forced him with the musket to drink the rest. How he had complied because he preferred to die of poisoning than to suffer an agonising death by musket-shot like his ancestor Walter von Baugenwitz. How the killer left the cellar confidently, how the baron in his death throes managed to lock the door from the inside and how the killer tried in vain to force it open to prevent her victim leaving a clue to her identity.

Angela understood for the first time why master detectives like Sherlock Holmes, Hercule Poirot or Miss Marple favoured long monologues at the end of their investigations. As a woman who loved efficiency, she had often wondered why fictional detectives made such a fuss of announcing the murderer. Why not just say, 'It was Colonel Mustard. With the candelabra. In the library'? But now Angela knew the answer: it was just so enjoyable to prolong the moment of revelation as she joined the ranks of those legendary detective. Sherlock Holmes, Hercule Poirot, Miss... Merkel?

Miss Merkel.

It sounded good.

'Why are you grinning like that?' asked the other Angela. 'Aren't we talking about murders here?'

Angela gave herself a severe mental reprimand. A master detective should not allow her thoughts to wander – and the fact that she'd been ticked off by that nasty woman made her lapse even worse. Pulling herself together, she said loudly and clearly, 'Before Philipp died he left a clue to the killer's identity.'

Angela brought out an A4 sheet of paper on which she had drawn the letter 'a'.

No one said a word.

'We'll come to what this means in a minute. For now, all I will say is that Alexa von Baugenwitz knew what it stood for. And that she was going to tell me in the church.'

'Hence,' said Pia, doing her best to sound bored, 'she had to be whacked?'

'Precisely. The killer had found out that we – my husband and I – had talked to Alexa in the castle that night and that Alexa had agreed to meet us in the church the following morning.'

'What were you doing in the castle at night?' asked the farmer.

'Alexa von Baugenwitz,' explained Achim helpfully, 'was about to make love with the Texan—'

'Do you actually call it "making love"?' grinned Pia.

'Yes, it's a very beautiful phrase.'

'It's lame.'

'You've got a cheek, young lady.'

'Don't let her wind you up, Muffin,' interrupted

231

Angela. The build-up to her exposure of the killer's identity wasn't going according to plan.

'Yes, Muffin,' said Pia mockingly, 'don't let me wind you up.'

Achim took a deep breath and straightened his back. 'As I was saying,' he continued, 'Alexa and the Texan were lying on the bed while Muff... Angela and I were lying beneath it.'

'That's way too perverted for me,' said Pia.

'It has nothing to do with perversion!'

'You keep telling yourself that.'

'You... you...'

'I... I...?'

'This is almost as bad as a party meeting!' said *Alternative für Deutschland* Angela. 'Can we please stick to the point?'

'Yes, enough!' said Katharina. 'If Philipp really was murdered, it must have been Alexa. The "a" he wrote is clearly the first letter of her name. And then, plagued by guilt, she threw herself from the church tower.'

'Like Adelheid von Baugenwitz?' asked Angela. 'After she'd killed her husband, Balduin the Butcher?'

'Exactly.'

'There's just one problem.'

'What might that be?'

'In the church we saw a person dressed in black, running away. Unfortunately we were unable to identify them. But later that morning I noticed that the glass lid on the cabinet containing the musket was in a different position from the day before. The killer used the weapon to force Alexa to climb the belltower and leap to her death, just as she'd forced Philipp to drink the hemlock.'

None of the women at the table said a word. They seemed to agree that the theory of Alexa's suicide was no longer tenable. At last Lena piped up. 'How did the killer hear you in the bedroom with Alexa? She must live in the castle – or she would never have found out.'

'I had the very same thought,' said Angela.

'That rules me out, then,' said the farmer, getting to her feet. 'I'll just grab another slice for the road.'

'Not so fast,' said Angela. 'After all, a non-resident of the castle could have found a way in. Through a secret passage, for example.' Angela gave Marie a friendly smile to try to signal that she wasn't a suspect. The young woman was still holding her tummy. 'But there's only one secret passage, and it doesn't lead into the wine cellar.'

'So not through a secret passage then?' said the other Angela irritably.

'No,' said Angela, looking at Lena. 'But perhaps some-body else knows weak spots in the castle's security.'

'There aren't any weak spots!' said Lena. 'I certified that for the insurance!' She looked towards Mike for help. But he, the consummate professional, showed no reaction.

'Yes, you did,' said Angela. 'But that's because you're in cahoots with Katharina von Baugenwitz!'

50

Lena and Katharina turned pale. The other Angela frowned. Marie looked agape. For a few seconds even Pia was unable to maintain her cool façade. Achim and Mike wore expressions of bewilderment. Angela hadn't told either the identity of the killer, only that she'd solved the case. She didn't want one of them acting in haste.

'Katharina von Baugenwitz,' said Angela, turning to her, 'your alibi for the death of your ex-husband comes from Lena.'

'Correct,' said Katharina, pulling herself together.

'Because you and Lena were inspecting the property together and confirmed that the castle fulfilled all the security requirements against a break-in.'

'That's also correct.' Katharina raised her chin as if to say: just you try to impugn me, you don't stand a chance.

'The fact is, however, the castle *is* vulnerable to a break-in, isn't it? And that explains why Lena fled the castle in horror on the night the baron was murdered.'

Lena went whiter, and tears came to her eyes.

'Tell the truth, Lena,' Mike said gently. The big man could no longer hide his feelings for her.

'It's not what you think!'

'It never is,' Angela said wisely, feeling more and more Sherlock-esque with every minute.

'This means Lena could have broken into the castle and overheard our conversation with Alexa von Baugenwitz!' cut in Achim, who for his part was feeling more and more Watson-ish.

'No, no! I swear I didn't! It wasn't like that at all!' The tears were running down Lena's cheeks.

Mike was torn between the urge to take her in his arms and his professional duty to apprehend her on suspicion of firing arrows at his boss.

'No, it wasn't like that,' said Angela, to everyone's surprise. 'It wasn't Lena who eavesdropped when we were talking to Alexa.'

'I get the whole Sherlock vibe you're going for,' said Pia, 'but are we going to find out who did it, like, some time this century?'

'It was, in fact, a resident of the castle,' said Angela, ignoring Pia and turning to her mother. 'Wasn't it, Katharina von Baugenwitz?'

Katharina said nothing. Instead the other Angela piped up. 'I hate to say it, but Frau von Baugenwitz can't have killed Alexa – she was in the field with me. I told you yesterday, when you were on my tractor.'

'Indeed you did.' Angela was smiling enigmatically.

'Surely you can't think all three of us are in cahoots?!'

Achim Watson stepped in. 'All three of you have a motive,' he said. 'You don't want your land to be sold off. Not to mention the fact that Philipp broke your heart. As for Lena, Philipp shot her while he was hunting, shattering her Olympic dream – then he wouldn't even cough up for the operation. And Frau von Baugenwitz wanted revenge after he abandoned her for Alexa.'

As Angela watched her husband roll out the *Murder-on-the-Orient-Express* theory, she reflected that, just like the great detectives, she had somebody at her side who was extremely capable yet only 90 per cent in the picture. An assistant who was forever one step off the pace, drawing the obvious but wrong conclusions. Holmes and Watson. Miss Marple and Mr Stringer. Miss Merkel and Mr Muffin.

'Just look at her – she's grinning again!' snarled her namesake. 'While I'm being accused of being part of a complicity!'

'You mean conspiracy,' said Achim. 'Not complicity.'

The farmer raised her fists and moved towards Achim, who took a rapid step back. Mike cleared his throat threateningly at the farmer.

'Yeah? Come on, then!' she said to the bodyguard, but without much conviction. It was clear she didn't really want Mike to take her up on it.

'Seriously?' said Pia. 'Do you believe the three of them were working together?'

'Do you know *Murder on the Orient Express*?' asked Achim.

'Is that a film?'

Angela decided the time had come to move beyond the *Orient Express* hypothesis. 'That's not what happened, Muffin.'

'But you said that Lena and Katharina von Baugenwitz were in cahoots.'

'And that's true. But only in a specific way.' She turned to Lena. 'You received 25,000 euros from Frau von Baugenwitz so you could have your shoulder operation. Am I right?'

'Yes.' Lena began weeping uncontrollably. Mike went

over to her. His first impulse was to take Lena in his arms and comfort her, but he checked himself.

After a deep breath Angela said, 'Only one person committed the murders.'

'Only one? But what about the *Orient Ex—*' said Achim, nonplussed.

'Muffin?'

'Yes, Muffinella?'

'Please let me finish.'

The tension around the table was now so high that even Pia refrained from making a snarky comment about the nicknames.

Angela now addressed Katharina. 'My husband has already mentioned one motive you may have had for the murders. But there are 200 million further motives. Aren't there, Frau von Baugenwitz?'

Katharina said nothing.

'You never wanted Philipp to sell the castle. Instead you wanted him to sue the German state for the restitution of his family's possessions, valued at 200 million euros. You even commissioned historians to write reports to bolster your case. Unlike you, however, Philipp couldn't care less about his family's history. He was happy with the money he'd get from the sale of the castle.'

'All of that is true,' admitted Katharina. 'Philipp was a fool. The government wouldn't have stood a chance against us. We would have been able to prove that Philipp's grandfather hadn't collaborated with the Nazis.'

'Prove, or merely obfuscate the connection to the extent that it was impossible to distinguish the truth from lies?'

'These days there's no difference.'

'Sadly that's true,' sighed Angela.

'Much as I'd like to continue this little philosophical debate, let's get back to the point,' said Katharina. 'Before marrying Philipp, I was stupid enough to sign a pre-nup. As his ex-wife I don't get a penny, let alone the 200 million you seem so interested in.'

'It's true. You don't get any of the money.'

'As I said.' Katharina smiled triumphantly.

'Not you. But your daughter...'

51

Everyone looked at Pia. But only for a moment because the great detective now said, 'And little Adrian.'

'Who the hell is Adrian?' asked the other Angela.

'My son...' gasped Marie.

'Oh, for fuck's sake. Why should your brat suddenly get the land I work my arse off to cultivate?'

'Illegitimate children have a statutory share,' explained Achim Watson.

'But why would I inherit anything from him?' said Pia. 'I'm just an ex-stepdaughter, aren't I?'

'That's what I thought at first – that you wouldn't have a claim because after the divorce you were no longer Philipp von Baugenwitz's stepdaughter.'

'Exactly.'

'But the fact is that you still are his stepdaughter.'

Pia looked at her mother. And Angela could plainly see that for the first time the girl seemed a little helpless.

For a long time Katharina was silent. Finally, she said, 'Philipp formally adopted Pia when she was small. Which means she stays his daughter forever. Even in the event of a divorce. But she didn't know! Philipp and I agreed that she should never find out about the adoption – she'd adored her real father and I never wanted her to feel that Philipp was meant to replace him.'

'This just gets better and better,' said the other Angela. 'Not only does the little bastard inherit something, but this minx too.'

'Ow!' Marie said, clutching her tummy again.

Angela prayed the contractions were not about to start. The verbal abuse must be causing Marie a good deal of stress. Or was it the revelation that her child was going to inherit more than a million euros? Both, no doubt. Angela resisted the urge to take her namesake to task. She had to stay ruthlessly focused!

'Katharina von Baugenwitz,' she said in her most authoritative tone, the one she'd kept in reserve for dealing with Boris Johnson. 'Did you kill your ex-husband Philipp von Baugenwitz and his wife Alexa?'

Katharina turned to look at her daughter, who gave her an imploring look. Taking a deep breath, she replied, 'Yes, I did.'

For a few moments everyone at the table just sat there without uttering a word. Then the silence was broken by the other Angela. 'Well, now I can finally go home,' she said, getting up.

'Not so fast,' said Achim. 'This makes you an accessory to murder.'

'How?'

'You gave her an alibi.'

'Erm... yes...' said the farmer, confused. 'But she really was with me when Alexa was killed... How can that be possible?'

'Well, I think we can all agree that we haven't got to the end of the story yet,' said Angela. 'There is still the matter of this piece of paper.' She flourished before them the A4 sheet which Philipp had scrawled on just before his death. 'Because "α" certainly does not stand for Katharina.'

52

'What does it stand for then?' asked farmer Angela.

'Do hashtags mean anything to you?'

'No, thank God.'

'Well, the last time I was in the wine cellar Pia started talking about hashtags. Isn't that right, Pia?'

'Whatever,' said the teenager.

'When she mentioned hashtags, my gut feeling told me there was some connection to Philipp's clue. Unfortunately, however, my gut feeling didn't tell me what it was.'

'But I've already confessed!' said Katharina. 'Why do we have to go on listening to your long, self-important explanations!'

'It's true, you confessed. But you still have two alibis.'

'I bribed her with 25,000 euros.' Katharina pointed at Lena. 'That's why she gave me an alibi.'

The policewoman was crying softly. 'My entire career, everything I've built up... my life...'

'Frau von Baugenwitz did indeed give Lena 25,000 euros,' said Angela to the assembled company. 'But the money wasn't to purchase an alibi. It was for a false declaration to the insurance company that the castle met the required security standards. A snip of the six-figure sum it would have cost to actually make the changes. And because Lena urgently needed the money for her operation, so she could finally be rid of the hellish pain in her shoulder and maybe have another try at the Olympics, she accepted the offer and made a deal on the very evening of the murder.' Angela gave the young policewoman a sympathetic look. 'But soon afterwards she was plagued by her bad conscience, which explains why she looked so upset when she left the castle courtyard. And it's still eating you up, isn't it, Lena?'

'I should never have done it!'

'No, you shouldn't have.'

Mike found the sight of Lena heart-rending. Angela tuned to him and said, 'Go on, give her a hug.'

'She knew nothing about the murders?'

'No, she just allowed herself to be bribed in a moment of weakness.'

Squatting beside Lena, Mike put a comforting arm around her.

'I don't know what this is all about,' said Katharina von Baugenwitz, 'but I'll tell you one thing for sure: the police are going to hear quite a different story from me!'

'No doubt they will,' said Angela. 'But you are forgetting about the hashtag. You see, now I know what my subconscious was trying to tell me.'

241

'What?' asked Achim.

'The hashtag is a symbol rather than a letter. Just like this "a". Once again Angela held up the sheet of A4. 'This isn't a letter either, but a symbol. And what it represents is—'

'AAARGH!'

Everybody turned to Marie, who sat with her eyes wide open, her face contorted with pain and sweat on her brow.

'The baby!' she said. 'It's coming!'

53

The grand reveal would have to wait. Right now there was something even more important than murder: new life!

Angela asked Mike to make sure that nobody left the garden. Then she led Marie into the bedroom and helped her lie down on her and Achim's bed. The contractions had started in earnest.

'I'm going to call an ambulance to get you to hospital,' said Angela.

'No, no – not hospital, there isn't time. The midwife's birthing centre is closer.'

'How close?'

'Twenty kilometres away, maybe... It's in Templin,' said Marie, before the next contraction came.

Angela went over to the window that overlooked the garden and called out, 'Mike, get the car ready! We have to take Marie to Templin. Right now!'

'Er... well... um,' stammered the bodyguard, who was holding the inconsolable Lena in his arms.

242

'Why do I get the feeling that I'm not going to like what I'm about to hear?'

'Because you won't.'

'So what is it?'

'The car isn't charged. I'm sorry, I forgot after all the hoo-ha yesterday.'

Angela returned to Marie, who was in the midst of another contraction. 'We'll have to go to hospital.'

'Please… call my midwife,' panted Marie once the contraction had passed. 'Tell her to come here.' She pressed the number and handed Angela her mobile.

As she held the phone to her ear, Angela wondered whether she should try again to convince Marie to go to hospital, despite the risk that the child might be born in the ambulance. But surely a mother had the right to decide where to give birth. Even if that place was Angela's bedroom.

'Brunsen,' said a woman with a very deep voice at the other end of the line.

'Hello, this is Angela Merkel.'

'Of course it is.'

'Please don't hang up!'

'I doubt Angela Merkel needs a midwife.'

'It really is me! Can't you tell by my voice?'

'Even my six-year-old grandson can imitate that.'

'I'm calling on behalf of Marie Horstmann. Your screen should be displaying her name.'

Angela held the mobile next to Marie just as she emitted another moan, then said, 'Please – there's no way we can get to the birthing centre. You have to come!'

243

'Please!' cried Marie.

'Alright, alright. I'm not far from Klein-Freudenstadt. Text me the exact address and I'll come over,' said Frau Brunsen, hanging up.

Marie managed a half-smile of relief. Angela sat beside her on the edge of the bed. 'Everything's going to be fine,' she said.

'How can you know that? At this very moment in the garden there's a killer who will stop at nothing to get her hands on Philipp's inheritance. And my little one... my little baby... is an heir.'

Angela had to admit the situation wasn't ideal. On the other hand, the killer would soon be under arrest. And meanwhile Mike was a very large and well-trained man. 'You mustn't worry,' she said, taking Marie's hand.

'Are you sure everything will be fine?' asked Marie.

In a clear, firm voice, Angela repeated the words that had once changed Europe but now seemed somehow even more important: 'We can do this!'

54

As soon as the sturdy, weather-beaten midwife who went by the name of Brunsen came storming into Angela's half-timber house, she gave a number of orders about what she needed for the birth. Angela and Achim got everything together and were now standing beside the bed.

'What are you two still doing here?' she barked.

'I was wondering the same thing,' said Achim, making a speedy exit.

'I promised Marie I'd be at the birth,' said Angela.

'That's very good of you. But the surroundings here are not as sterile as in the birthing centre.' The midwife turned to Marie. 'It really would be better if the two of us did this on our own.'

Marie, bathed in sweat, nodded briefly. Angela was surprised to feel a touch of disappointment. She would have thought she'd feel relieved not to have to be at the birth. But she smiled at Marie and said, 'You can do this!'

Then she went back out into the garden, where the other Angela, her mouth full of a third slice of chocolate cake, greeted her: 'At last! Can we finally bring this to an end?'

'Yes,' said Angela, though her mind was still on Marie so she said nothing more for a while.

'I mean, today!'

'Yes, of course,' Angela said, pulling herself together. 'Now, where was I?'

'You were saying something about how it's a symbol, not a letter.'

'Precisely!' Angela was back on track. It was time to deliver the great coup of her investigation. 'Philipp von Baugenwitz's clue to the identity of the killer is a symbol. I realised that yesterday when I was writing an email.'

'Newsflash! Angela Merkel knows what an email is,' said Pia.

'Watch carefully,' said Angela, ignoring this. She took a pen and began drawing a loop around the 'a'. Then she held up the paper, on which was now written:

'Philipp died before he could draw the circle around the letter,' she explained.

There was a general murmur of surprise. Only Katharina von Baugenwitz seemed unmoved.

Angela turned to her. 'You always knew what it meant, didn't you? That's why you were so shocked when I drew the letter in the gravel.'

'I thought it stood for Alexa,' said Katharina acidly.

'No, you didn't.'

'So what's your theory? That Philipp was going to write an entire email – on a piece of paper – just before he died?'

'No. He sensed he had very little time left. So he chose this symbol as the shortest possible clue to the killer. Not because of its use in emails but on social media, like—'

'Instagram!' said Achim.

All eyes turned to Pia.

55

'How many times do I have to tell you?' said Katharina in desperation. 'It… was… ME!'

'You have alibis. And whatever you say, they're watertight.'

Katharina looked miserably at Pia.

'The first time we met,' continued Angela, 'you told me you'd do anything for your daughter.'

'Yes,' came the meek reply.

'Does that include confessing to murders you haven't committed?'

Katharina didn't answer.

246

'When you found the door to the wine cellar locked on the night of the first murder you panicked. Because you knew full well what your daughter was capable of.'

Still no answer.

'And you also realised at once that Pia had faked Philipp's suicide. So you thought on your feet and while we were still in the cellar told me that your ex-husband had been tired of life.'

Katharina lowered her eyes.

Angela turned to Pia. 'As for you, it was the inheritance you wanted.'

'Have you forgotten?' said Pia with a coldness that caused Achim to faintly shudder. 'I've got a livestream as an alibi.'

'I took another look at that last night.' Angela pulled an iPad from her Longchamp bag and played the clip of the wine festival that Pia had filmed for her followers. In it, the blue-haired teenager was making fun of the guests. She called the Macarena dance 'arhythmic gymnastics'. She remarked about Philipp in full armour, 'That's what comes of centuries of inbreeding.' And, at the end of her video, bent over the half-empty bowl of Baugenwitz punch, she said, 'Paint stripper is the nectar of the gods compared to this stuff. Now I know why I get bevved up on Dom Perignon. So should you! And don't forget: anarchy is possible, if you can get it organised!'

'The timecode proves that I was at the festival when Philipp was murdered in the cellar,' said Pia.

'It would do,' said Angela, 'if it weren't faked. You thought that neither the inspector nor I would ever notice.

247

Because us fogies don't have a clue about social media.'

Pia couldn't withhold a scornful grin.

'And it's true, I didn't consider the possibility until I'd understood what the symbol was about.'

'Did you have the video checked by IT specialists?' asked Achim.

'That wasn't necessary.'

'How come?'

'Do you remember sampling the last glass of punch?'

'Unfortunately, yes,' said Achim with another shudder. 'Revolting stuff. What about it?'

'Well, in the video Pia is standing by a half-full bowl. And that means she must have taken her film long before the murder took place.'

'So she doesn't have an alibi!' said Achim Watson.

'The police IT experts will be able to confirm that the timecode was faked.' Angela turned back to Pia. 'Unfortunately for you, you weren't able to fashion a second alibi after Alexa's death. You had to hope that the one for the first murder would suffice. Particularly as the police thought it was suicide.'

Pia narrowed her eyes.

'And if somebody – a hobby detective, for example – unexpectedly got onto you, you could always rely on a mother's love to protect you.'

Pia's eyes were now full of hatred; Katharina collapsed in her chair.

'Ever since the accident your mother caused, in which your father died, she's had such a bad conscience that she'd do everything for you, as you well know.'

248

Now the tears came to Katharina von Baugenwitz's eyes.

'It was in order to protect you that your mother claimed you didn't know Philipp had adopted you, making you his heir. All lies!' Angela turned to Katharina. 'Isn't that so, Frau von Baugenwitz? Your daughter knew about the adoption. She knew she would inherit.'

Katharina gave the faintest of nods. She was a broken woman.

'You would have let your mother go to prison for you!'

Pia ignored this. 'Right now I'm earning shitloads with my postings,' she said. 'But this sort of thing never lasts. It could be all over in two years. What then? I mean, I never even finished school. And my adoptive father was planning to abscond with his bitch, leaving mum and me without a penny. And we were going to get all the property back!'

'At a value of 200 million euros.'

'It wasn't just about the money, but the family name as well!'

'And as his adoptive daughter you're one of them.'

'Yes – much more than Philipp, who couldn't give a shit about any of it! We would have made the von Baugenwitzes great again. As great as in the past!'

'Like under the Nazis.'

'And under Balduin the Butcher!'

'So you are interested in history.'

'Of course I am! Only fools aren't.'

'Your mother mentioned how you spent your childhood in the castle library. It was there that you read up on the family history, so that you knew precisely how to

249

make the murders of Philipp and Alexa look like echoes of the past.'

'I got a kick out of that!'

'And you also used the past to divert suspicion onto Alexa.'

'If anybody got the idea it was murder, the historical similarities meant she'd be the first person they'd think of. And reckon she'd killed herself afterwards – just like with Adelheid and Balduin in the seventeenth century.'

'And no doubt the idea of shooting at me with the crossbow also came from your love of the past?'

'That gave me the biggest kick of all!'

'You admit everything, then?'

'No point in denying it now.'

'Don't you have any regrets?'

'None.'

'You'll be put away for a long time for a double murder plus an attempted murder.'

'Not if I can help it.'

'No?'

'I'll go down for a triple murder.' Pia reached into the bag on the ground beside her chair, pulled out the musket and aimed it straight at Angela.

56

It had been a strange day for Putin. For the dog, that is, rather than the Russian president. Unlike his namesake, four-legged Putin was focused on the things that mattered: food, sleep and being stroked. They filled his life

250

completely. On this day, however, all the things he liked were being seriously neglected. Instead of making a fuss of him as she usually did, his mistress was talking to a bunch of other women, not a single one of whom had been kind enough to drop even a morsel from the sumptuously laid table. Although in the depths of his pug brain Putin knew that the sweet morsels weren't good for his tummy, they tasted so delicious! Surely someone could have shared a bit of theirs with him! 'Scandal' was the word, if only Putin's vocabulary had been large enough to know it.

And to add insult to injury, now that he'd just lain on a soft patch of lawn to enjoy a doze in the sunshine, all the humans were suddenly flustered. With a deep snort-sigh, he lifted his head to see what was going on. The woman with the weird hair was pointing a stick at his mistress. Was she going to throw the stick so his mistress could run off and fetch it? Putin couldn't remember his mistress ever retrieving a stick before – it was something he, Putin, loved to do. A couple of times at any rate; after that he found it too tiring. But now he noticed that his mistress seemed to be frightened of the stick. How strange! The other humans were frightened of it too, especially his master who was giving off a powerful smell of terror. Wait… did this mean that his mistress was in danger?

The pug leapt up, took a sniff with his flat nose, and thought: *I smell fear and anger in the air*. The anger was streaming from the woman with the stick, the fear from everyone else. The tall man called Mike, who Putin really liked because he always shared his toast and liver sausage with him, took a step towards the woman with the weird hair. But she pointed the stick at him and he stopped. If even the huge liver-sausage man was frightened of the stick then it definitely wasn't a game of fetch being played here.

The woman with the weird hair pointed the stick at his mistress again. Then she said some words the pug didn't understand. This wasn't surprising, since he couldn't understand most things humans said, only a few such as 'Foodies', 'Treats' and 'You're such a sweet little mouse'. Whereas the words the woman had spoken were: 'I'm going to prison anyway. I might as well get myself written into the history books while I'm at it!'

His mistress was now terrified – Putin could smell it, even though she was trying not to let it show.

His mistress mustn't die!

Why was nobody doing anything?

Now the woman with the weird hair aimed the stick at his mistress's face.

Stupid shit-woman!

Putin wondered whether to bark. But he knew full well that nobody took his barking seriously. Least of all the silly cat across the street.

Putin saw only one way to save his mistress. He raced over and bit the woman right in the calf!

She screamed. The liver-sausage man ran over and pulled her to the ground. As she fell she dropped the stick. Putin grabbed it with his mouth – it was very heavy and tasted odd too – and brought it to his mistress. She took the stick and gave him a loving pat on the head. 'Well done, Putin,' she said. 'You saved the day!' She was beaming at him even more fondly than the time when as a puppy he'd first done his business outside the house.

Even though the pug couldn't quite work out what had just happened, at that moment Putin was prouder of himself than ever before.

57

Angela stood on the small cobbled street by the police car in which Pia sat, handcuffed. Beside her, Inspector Hannemann leaned with his hands against the car roof and let out the deepest sigh Angela had ever heard him or anyone else make. 'It seems you were right after all,' he said quietly.

'It certainly does,' said Angela. The shock was still in her limbs but had been joined by another feeling: pride. She had solved the case! The important thing now was not to crow in front of the inspector. No matter how hard that was. It was not the done thing in victory.

'And now I'm going to look as stupid in the eyes of my superiors as I already do to my ex-wife.'

'Not necessarily.'

'What do you mean?'

'The two of us can pretend you solved the case.'

'We can?'

'That way the press will never find out and I'll have my peace and quiet.'

'But—'

'Nobody at the station in Templin knows any different. Apart from Lena, and she has her own reasons to
keep quiet.'

'What reasons are they?'

'Do you really want to know? Or would you rather
play the hero?'

'Hero sounds better.'

'That's what I thought. Pia and the farmer might blab
about my involvement, but who is going to pay attention? This is Klein-Freudenstadt, after all, not Berlin or
Brussels.'

Hannemann was barely able to believe his luck. 'This
will be the greatest success of my career!'

'I'm delighted for you.'

'Maybe there's still the chance of a promotion at my age.'

'Nothing's impossible.'

'And then my ex-wife might come back to me.'

'Don't get your hopes up too much.'

'You're right,' said Hannemann. 'That isn't going to
happen. Can I make one final request.'

'What's that?'

'Please never meddle again in police investigations.
Particularly not when it's a case of murder.'

'My dear Inspector Hannemann,' Angela said with a
broad grin, 'I'm afraid that's a promise I cannot make.'

58

By the time Angela had returned to the garden, Katharina von Baugenwitz and the other Angela had long gone.

One a broken woman, the other in outrage at the fact that her landlord would henceforth be Marie. This fact gave Angela great pleasure.

As for Marie, they could hear her cries of pain despite the closed bedroom windows. Out of respect for the poor woman's privacy, Mike, Lena and Achim had retired to the furthest corner of the garden. Beside them in the grass lay Putin, whom Achim had rewarded with an extra-large bone and Mike with some liver-sausage on toast. When Angela joined them Achim said, 'You really are a Sherlockella and I'm proud to be your Watson.'

Angela wasn't sure they truly deserved these accolades. But she kept her thoughts to herself and instead gave him a loving kiss on the cheek. 'You are a wonderful husband,' she said.

'Thanks. You are too.'

'I'm a wonderful husband?' asked Angela playfully, then quickly turned to Lena before he could reply. The policewoman's eyes were red and swollen with crying.

'I made it clear to Hannemann that he's not to undertake any investigation into you. So nobody's going to punish you for the bribery.'

'Nobody apart from myself,' Lena said softly.

'Don't be so hard on yourself,' Mike said, trying to put an arm around her.

'Don't,' she said, moving away.

'What's wrong?'

'I'm going to go to my aunt's in Berlin. I need to get my head in order.'

'When will you be back?'

Lena didn't reply.

'You are coming back, aren't you?'

Again, no reply.

'Lena?'

'I don't know.' She stood up and turned to Angela. 'Thank you.'

'My pleasure.'

As Lena walked away Mike sighed quietly. 'This isn't quite how I'd imagined our third date.'

Angela put a friendly hand on his elbow. 'You'll find happiness,' she said. 'I'm certain of it.'

Mike gave the faintest of smiles.

'And until you do, tuck in. There's plenty of cake left over.'

Mike groaned. 'If I carry on like this only women with a fetish for fat men will even look at me.'

But before he had a chance to bite into the cake, Achim said, 'Do you hear that?'

The other two listened intently.

'I can't hear anything,' said Mike.

'Me neither,' said Angela.

'Exactly!' grinned Achim.

Angela understood. 'Marie!'

'She must've had the baby!' said Achim.

Angela felt more jittery than she'd ever been in Klein-Freudenstadt. And given the events of the past few days that was saying something. She hoped everything had gone smoothly, that both mother and child were well!

At that moment the midwife stepped into the garden. 'Marie and Adrian would like to see you now!' she called.

59

Marie was lying in the bed the midwife had freshly made. She held her brand-new baby, wrapped in a small blanket. Angela wouldn't have thought it possible that someone could look so worn out and yet so happy at the same time.

'I'll leave you alone for now,' said Frau Brunsen. 'I've had an emergency call that I must attend to. But don't worry, Marie, I'll look in again afterwards.'

'Thank you.'

'Besides, you've got someone else to look after you,' said the midwife, smiling at the lady of the house.

'Yes,' said Marie happily. 'I suppose I have.'

As soon as Frau Brunsen had left, Angela moved over to the bed and gazed at the sleeping baby. He looked just like his mother.

'Would you like to hold him?' said Marie.

'What, who, me?' said Angela in surprise.

'Can you see anyone else in the room?'

'No.' All of a sudden Angela felt unsure in a way that was totally new to her.

'Come on, then,' said Marie.

Angela sat hesitantly on the edge of the bed. Marie passed her the little bundle and Angela held it as tensely as she might a raw egg.

'Relax, he's not a nuclear bomb.'

It was easier said than done.

'Hold him to your chest if you like.'

Angela did what she was told. It felt wonderful. She could even feel the little one's heartbeat. And a teardrop of emotion welled in her eye. When was the last time that had happened? When Achim proposed to her decades ago. At that time she'd only just been able to stop herself from bawling out of sheer happiness.

To distract herself Angela said, 'Little Adrian is really sweet.'

'He has another name.'

'How do you mean?'

'I've named him after you.'

'Angela?' said Angela. She was puzzled. She'd always known that after her death the odd airport or station would probably be named after her, but it had never once crossed her mind that anyone might name their living child after her. Also, she wondered whether calling the boy Angela was a good idea. Even if it was only his middle name, wouldn't he be teased mercilessly?

'No, you silly-billy,' laughed Marie.

'Surely you don't mean Merkel?'

Marie was laughing so much she could hardly speak. She shook her head.

'What, then?'

'Ángel,' she said.

Now it was Angela's turn to lose her voice.

'It's Spanish for angel.'

Angela looked down at the little Adrian Ángel asleep in her arms. Now she couldn't help herself; she let the tears flow. And as she wept, she thought, Klein-Freudenstadt, you are a place of miracles!

Acknowledgements

My great, no, what am I saying, my immense thanks go to my wonderful editor Ulrike Beck for accompanying me on all the paths I've gone down. Thanks are also due to my mentor Michael Töteberg, who read this book like a serial, chapter by chapter as I was writing it, and encouraged me all the way. And, Angela Merkel, thank you too.